G000113049

About the Author

Mark Bashford lives quietly in West Wales where he divides his time between family, friends, model cars, travelling to Europe and China, taking walks and writing books when the weather is bad. *From Benefits To Billions* is his first contemporary novel. Others are in planning.

From Benefits to Billions

Mark Bashford

From Benefits to Billions

Olympia Publishers
London

www.olympiapublishers.com
OLYMPIA PAPERBACK EDITION

Copyright © Mark Bashford 2019

The right of Mark Bashford to be identified as author of
this work has been asserted in accordance with sections 77 and 78
of the Copyright, Designs and Patents Act 1988.

All Rights Reserved

No reproduction, copy or transmission of this publication
may be made without written permission.
No paragraph of this publication may be reproduced,
copied or transmitted save with the written permission of the
publisher, or in accordance with the provisions
of the Copyright Act 1956 (as amended).

Any person who commits any unauthorised act in relation to
this publication may be liable to criminal
prosecution and civil claims for damage.

A CIP catalogue record for this title is
available from the British Library.

ISBN: 978-1-78830-444-3

This is a work of fiction.
Names, characters, places and incidents originate from the writer's
imagination. Any resemblance to actual persons, living or dead, is
purely coincidental.

First Published in 2019

Olympia Publishers
60 Cannon Street
London
EC4N 6NP

Printed in Great Britain

Dedication

For those who help and those who helped. Both near and far.
You know who you are. Thank you.

Take-Off
London Airport Private Runway

Mark Bashford and his beautiful French wife Elisabeth huddled together in a vain attempt to shield themselves and their two children, Angelina and Roland, from the merciless wind that was blowing contrary to them as they made their way all too slowly across the tarmac to the Forward Cover Insurance, Inc. company jet. This was an uncommon experience for them. The jet was Mark's personal absolute favourite boy-toy of all, and normally they would have arrived in plenty of time, at least two hours allowing Elisabeth and the two children to raid the shops, after checking in, without any restraint, then board the jet via the covered walk-way provided by the airport. But this morning had been different. This morning, Roland had been sick and bad-tempered the whole time. So much so, in fact, that Elisabeth, seeing the situation getting completely out of hand when Angelina decided to join in, laid down the ultimatum of cancelling their proposed business trip to Florida. The moment she had given voice to this dire possibility was, of course, the very same moment when both children began to make miraculous recoveries. This now meant that they had to rush for their lives to the jet, or they would lose their window for take-off, and, because today was for the tower one of their busiest days, had no idea when another would be provided. Added to that was the undiminished protests from the eight-year-old Angelina when she was told firmly that there was no time for shopping, meaning that both Mark and Elisabeth were on the edge of their collective tethers, when at last a staircase truck overtook them heading in the same direction towards the jet and screeched to a halt directly in front of them. They did not bother thinking why they had not boarded the truck at departure. It was just too good seeing it. They all climbed inside and sat down thankfully. On arrival directly underneath Mark's personal boarding entrance, and without so much as a word to the driver, Elisabeth ushered the two children onto the staircase and then clambered unceremoniously up behind them, and Mark pressed the big red button at the bottom to get the stairs moving. Elisabeth and the two children laughed.

"At last we are on our way!" she shouted down to him, trying to make herself heard over the wind and the roar of the jet's engines. Mark laughed and shook his head, amazed.

"Get a move on, all of you! We're not even on board yet!"

As the door opened out to them, it was the children's turn to cheer. Not content to sit still on the moving stairs anymore, they scrambled to the top, where Sue the stewardess helped them inside, hugged them both warmly, and ushered them to their seats. Then, because she simply could not resist it, poked her head outside into the wind and noise.

"Come on, you two! You're holding us up!"

But before either Mark or Lizzy could reply, they were at the top and safely inside. Elisabeth joined the children without a word. Of course, as soon as they were inside, everyone wanted to go to the bathroom. Mark banged twice on the internal door to the cockpit with the heel of his left fist.

"Ready when you are, Paul!"

"Glad you could join us!" he shouted back. Mark shook his head and smiled again, without answering, and took his seat in the family saloon, where he found himself alone. He knew better than to sit at a window. That was strictly the children's domain.

"Sue! Andy! Please carry out all security checks. Take-off in precisely eight point five minutes and counting," came Paul's voice over the speaker. He was in Captain mode, now.

"Good morning, Mark. What will it be? Whisky or brandy?" asked Andy, who had appeared genie-like, as always, at his right shoulder.

"It'll be black coffee this morning, thank you, Andy. We'll save the booze until later when the children are asleep, huh?" He always meant to ask his old friend and steward how he was able to silently appear and disappear as he did. It was uncanny. Had he spent some years in the Tibetan mountains, or something? It was an idle thought. He dismissed it.

He waited for nothing in particular, grateful for a small moment's peace. Lizzy brought the children back from the bathroom to sit with him. Judging from the length of time they had taken, and the pinched expressions on the children's faces, some strong words had been spoken, probably something along the lines of informing them that they had better be on their best behaviour or they would stay in the hotel room the whole time with only their homework for company. He smiled and laughed silently at them. This is how well he knew them. At the sight of his smile, Roland came running.

"Come on, big guy!" Mark called, "you can make it!" And without another word, the child was on his lap, clinging to him, arms around his waist. Mark lifted him up, hugged him and playfully ruffled his hair.

"Aw, Dad!" Roland protested, "Mum just combed me!"

"Uh-oh! Do you think I'm in trouble, now?"

He hugged his father a little tighter and made big eyes in his mother's direction. Mark laughed.

"That bad, huh?" Roland replied with silence. Mark laughed again.

"Well, it simply means that we're all gonna have to be good, right? Besides, Mum's our warrior queen and we wouldn't have it any other way." He waited in silence. Lizzy smiled back at them all. Mark continued smiling back, but as he stared at her, he recalled the unforgettable moment they first met, and his smile changed its texture. "I wouldn't have it any other way, that's for sure," he said in a lower, husky tone.

"What's a ghoul?" asked Angelina loudly, looking up from her tablet, which she had been reading since they had sat down together. Mark thought that even at the age of eight, she was mature enough to know how to change the subject and the course of any conversation. She was definitely headed for great things.

"Come round this side of the table and sit next to me. We're about to take off," answered Lizzy in a clipped voice, before another word could be said. Angelina sighed and rolled her eyes at not getting an answer, but obeyed.

"A ghoul is a monster," Lizzy finally said when her daughter slumped down into the seat between her and the window, "and why are you reading a horror story? They're depressing and we're on holiday."

"I'm not reading a horror story." Angelina insisted. "I'm reading what people are saying about Dad."

"Then you're doing more than me," Mark said, raising his voice. "I never read that rubbish. Do as your mother says. I agree. We're on holiday."

Again, without another word, Angelina slid the tablet into the magazine holder down the right-hand side of her seat and clipped her seat belt, pulling it as tight as it would allow so that the seat would not have to be adjusted to child setting – a thing her girlish vanity was dreading.

"Don't you think you had better go and say hello or something to the troops?" Lizzy said to Mark, when she was satisfied that her daughter had done as she was told. She motioned with a flick of her head to the area behind their family saloon.

"That's the kitchen. You mean you want me to go talk to Sue and Andy?" Mark joked, teasing her.

"They're the help. I mean the troops." answered Lizzy, her straight face signifying an awareness of his bait, but a clear refusal to rise. Time for all that later, no doubt, she thought.

"Oh, the troops! I forgot all about the *troops*! Wow! So sorry..." Mark looked down at Roland, who was already asleep, and slid him gently and slowly into the vacant seat next to him, hoping against hope that he would not wake up. Then he slowly clipped the seat belt and pulled it to. Success! With equal stealth he got up and sidled into the kitchen. As soon as he entered, Andy was on him.

"The coffee won't be long, but you heard the order. Security comes first. Sorry."

"Nothing to be sorry about," Mark whispered. He smiled and nodded and pointed at the closed curtains on the opposite side of the kitchen. Andy's eyes widened with sudden understanding.

"Oh right!" he also whispered, smiling back. Mark took hold of the two curtain handles and flung them apart as if with all the flourish of a seasoned stage performer. Applause and a loud noise was made from the sixteen waiting executives, each with their significant others, all chosen with the utmost care, who comprised the main governing body of Forward Cover Insurance, now Incorporated. For a private moment, and there had been many of them leading up to this point, it amazed him that this was even happening at all. He took a deep breath.

"Okay! Okay!" he shouted, raising and clapping both hands in a plea for at least temporary silence. "Great to see you all. We've come a long way, and now we finally get to take FCI to USA. Well done, all of you! Now tell me, are we all ready for a kick-ass vacation – oh, sorry, I mean of course conference meeting – in Florida?"

A huge roar and raising of glasses. Mark put his right hand behind his right ear as if trying to hear their reaction.

"I'm sorry! What was that?"

This time, it was almost deafeningly loud.

"Hey, Mark. Mark!" shouted Susan Foster, Deputy Team Leader. "You know, I think we could get rich out of this one!"

Everyone laughed.

"Take it easy, Susan. It's a long flight, and we haven't

even taken off yet, but I do think that there might be just a slim chance of that. Agreed?" he goaded back.

Another loud cheer.

"All right. Strap yourselves in, people. It's world-conquering time!" At the raucous cheering and applause, he bowed to them, closed the curtains and made a light-footed about-turn, expecting to see Andy, but instead seeing Sue standing silently, espresso in hand.

"You had better strap yourself in, too. We're almost taking off," she whispered, handing him the cup and saucer which he took, drinking its contents with one swallow. He smiled, wiped his mouth with the tiny cotton towel that hung over her right forearm, placed the crockery in her waiting hands and returned to his seat. She found herself relishing these little performances. Mark was convinced that the way she and Andy worked together, it was obvious that they had a thing. If that was so, he was happy for them, but it was for him a matter of small significance. He did not consider this a subject worth raising with Lizzy.

They were all quiet on his return. At first, he wondered if there had been more words of correction given, but as he sat down, he saw that both children were now asleep. He slid carefully into his seat next to his son and fastened his seat belt. Just then, he noticed that Angelina's tablet had fallen onto the floor in front of her. Of course, it couldn't stay there, so he stretched down to pick it up to put it away properly prior to take-off. It had only been his intention to glance at the screen when he remembered the question she had asked. Dad's voice was unmistakable, but Esprit Fort was the name he had given to his rage, and it was like the return of an old friend from years ago, with whom, with the runaway success of his business, he had lost contact. But as his intended glance turned into a stare when he read the words on the screen, his old friend stopped by to say hello.

Hello, me old mucker. Remember me? Of course you do! You said goodbye to me! You said you wanted nothing more to do with me! You said I was an embarrassment to you! But you do remember me though, don't you, eh? Otherwise I wouldn't be here, would I, heh? Well just remember this too, kiddo! This world will never be short of bastards who want to bring you down! It was a fight to get it, and it's a fight to keep it, and you never know who your next enemy is going to be! And that goes for your smoking hot trophy wife and those two adorable little kids of yours! This is a fight that will only finish when you're dead, and don't you ever forget it!

He was powerless against this onslaught.

"Mark? Is everything okay?" Lizzy asked. She had watched him as he read the tablet, grinding his teeth, but now he was breathless and sweating. Time to step in. He jerked his head to his left and stared at her, looking as if he had been struck by lightning. His face was wet with sweat, his eyes were wide and his bottom lip trembled.

"I love you," he gasped.

She reached out with both hands above the sleeping Roland and drew him closer, held his face in both hands and kissed him deeply, the salty taste of his sweat sending butterflies to her stomach. Mark angrily thrust the tablet into the magazine folder.

"As soon as we've taken off, I'm going for a shower. Care to join me?" Her first thought was that this would give Sue a much-needed rest as well as a chance to spend time with the children, whom she adored.

"If you insist," she answered with a savvy, one-sided grin. He nodded.

The law of lift met the power of thrust and the jet left the ground.

There was a cheer from the passenger saloon.

Just as they were taking off, he remembered that he had forgotten to power down the tablet before thrusting it into the holder. He didn't care. His old friend waited silently in the pit of his stomach at the thought of what was on the screen:

"What people are saying about Mark Bashford."

"A ghoul. The man should be locked up for even thinking such a thing in the first place. Really! How does he sleep at night?" Katie Singleton. Daily Junction Report.

"It's no surprise that he got mega rich. No one has ever thought of this sort of thing. Good luck to him." Oliver Bailey. Valley Post.

"Everyone is talking about Mark Bashford. And what is more, everyone wants to sign up, now that we have been *awakened*, as it were." Oscar Quinn. The Advocate.

"Breathing, sleeping and walking are the only things that we human beings get to do that do not involve a financial cost. I suppose that, soon, this man from nowhere is going to find a way of making money out of that too. Do we really want to live in such a world?" Amelia Webster. Abergamlas Guardian.

Abergamlas

My name is Mark Bashford. I was born on 18th July, 1951 in a small village called Abergamlas just outside Cardiff in South Wales. I am the only child of English parents, Dennis and Helen, who loved me and gave me a healthy and happy childhood. They brought me up to be well-mannered and always to have an upbeat, positive attitude to life. They were really great people. No, I was never abused in any way, neither mentally nor physically, nor indeed sexually. We had lots of fun together and were as much mates as family. Also, I enjoyed school, and made many good friends there. Sadly, because my parents bore their only child late in life, they passed away when I was quite young. I was only seventeen when my father died and twenty when my mother passed away. I have very fond memories of them and still miss them very much.

Hawkey's Dog

My Mum had a nickname for my father and that nickname was Hawkey. It was also the habit of everyone else who knew him to use that same nickname. In fact, I now admit that it was only until the day of his funeral that I actually discovered that his name was Dennis. That is something truly amazing to me even at this time in life, don't you think? And as to the reason for this state of affairs? Why he was decorated with such a prestigious *nom de plume*? It is at the time of writing unknown to me. He was not particularly sharp-eyed, while neither on the other hand was he visually impaired. For example, he never wore spectacles, and he had two eyes, as opposed to only one.

But my father was definitely a man's man. He bred dogs. But these were not the type of animal you would look at and say something like, "Ah! Nice puppy!" No, if you saw one of *my* father's dogs, you would probably take a few involuntary steps back, say absolutely nothing and leave very quickly. These dogs were all muscle, teeth and rage.

You see, he bred dogs for fighting – a so-called sport that has since been very rightly outlawed.

But what can you say about these animals? This was their only reason for existing. These terrible events (to which I give not even the merest passive nod of approval) took place in a derelict building outside our village behind what was called "the forestry" known as the Old Pit Head Baths. I was never allowed anywhere near this place, and that included the other nightmare that would have been the kennels as well. I don't know what happened to these animals after my father went ill. Probably one of his mates took over. I don't know. But they must have been awful places. I have since heard many reports about it, and do not include any of them here because they were more like horror stories, what with the sound they made and all the blood and everything.

But my father felt sorry for one particular dog, and brought him home. He said that little Whitey wasn't tough enough for the pit – wouldn't have lasted a moment. And besides, it would be a good chance for me to get used to animals and it's always good for a boy to have a dog. Make a good companion for me, wouldn't he? Well, being the dutiful and obedient son of my father, I accepted his gift of a puppy. After all, little Whitey was nothing but an old softy, right?

Wrong! Little Whitey was the devil in a dog disguise!

All I can say is, and can only ever speculate on the truthfulness of the matter, because as I said, I was never allowed to go anywhere near the kennels, that if little Whitey was a softy, I only dread to think what the others must have been like!

He was one mean puppy!

And as for taking him out for walkies, forget about it. Little Whitey was totally self-sufficient. You might safely say that he made his own plans.

He would snap at all my friends, and bark at the neighbours, and you could tell that he enjoyed it, too! Yet the strange thing was, amazingly, everyone loved him! It was as if he had cast a spell over them or something. He was horrible, yet he would go into other people's houses, and they would feed him! Yes, that's right, the very neighbours whom he barked at would take pity on him and give him food!

"Ah, there you are, Whitey," they would say, or something like that. Then he would come home and expect to be fed again!

If he was human, Whitey would have been a gangster. I'm convinced of it!

At that time my Mum rented a huge black and white TV from the Co-Op. This was installed and placed on a small, low table under the living room window, facing the front of our house. My father was definitely not one for television until he went ill, and then my Mum bought him a colour TV. It was the late sixties and we were one of the first families in our village to own one. We would sit with him and watch together, and it would help to keep him calm. But in those early black and white days, my Mum used to enjoy the wrestling on a Saturday afternoon and I used to enjoy Blue Peter, my favourite childhood show.

But *little Whitey* put a quick and abrupt end to all my Blue Peter enjoyment! After a full day of eating out, he would come in and find me on the floor watching telly after school and sit himself down right in front of the screen and face me and just give me that evil stare of his, as if to say, "Yeah! Go on, cry! Just what do you think you're going to do about it?" baring his teeth and growling at me at the same time. There was of course nothing I *could* do about it, except wait for him to scramble off to the kitchen when he heard Mum opening a tin of meat. Later, I did that myself. It was dangerous business, let me tell you. I discovered what my poor old mother went through. I don't really think that my Mum really wanted him in the house, but, Hawkey gets what Hawkey wants, is what she kept telling me. Whitey would growl at me as the tin turned in its slow, anti-clockwise circle. When it stopped, he would continue with more growling and a few barks as I was putting the foul-smelling meat into his bowl. Then, as said bowl finally landed on the floor in front of him, he would bark even more loudly and I had to get out of his way as quickly as possible to avert his attempt to bite my hand off!

Then, one Christmas, my surprise present was a European Championship table soccer game, complete with a stadium, floodlights, and figures of the referee and linesmen, together with boxes of figures in the strips of all the major contending teams, hand painted to the most minute detail. It must have cost them an absolute fortune. I am now well known as a serious fan of the Beautiful Game, and that's how I got started!

But I refer to it as *table* soccer for the want of a better word, although that was the official name for it. This was because in practical terms it was impossible to give it the pride of place it richly deserved on any table that my parents owned. But me and my father together, on that never-to-be forgotten, comfortable, personally nostalgic childhood memory of a Christmas morning, set it up together (well, he did, mostly, you know how it is!) and played each other. We didn't take the part of one country or another, or anything. He was, like, Hawkey United, and I was something like Mark Athletic. Or something like that. I can't remember what the score was, now. Doesn't really matter, does it? My Mum was the ultimate referee, who whistled full time because our long-anticipated Christmas dinner was ready.

And that was little Whitey's big chance!

We had assembled the stadium in front of the television on the carpet on the uneven living room floor, because that was the largest open space available in our house, and as soon as we got up to go into the kitchen for dinner, the devil in a dog disguise, strangely not interested in food that particular day, came swaggering in and sat down on my new Euro Stadium, crushing half of it, including the Royal Box, one floodlight, and most of the figures. Even though I was only about eleven or so at the time, and Hawkey was a tough guy, I'm not ashamed to admit that I cried like a baby. And Hawkey agreed with me.

For him, that was the game-changer, with no apology for the pun. Yes, to his great credit, Hawkey went mental!

Shouting curses at the evil beast who was, in my opinion, getting a long deserved helping of justice, he grabbed Whitey by the collar and, holding him away from himself at arm's length (remember, he was an eating machine and by this time was now a very big dog), marched him out of the living room, through the kitchen where we had set up our dining table, out through the back door and out to the bottom of our long garden. What happened next was a sight to see; a real spectacle. This is the truth. My father literally drop-kicked the dog up the garden. My Mum screamed. She thought he had killed the poor animal. If I'm honest, it was the first time, but certainly not last, that I actually felt sorry for him. But not much, obviously. Whitey landed hard against the door of our garden shed, into which he scrambled as if his life depended on it. Had

Whitey at last learned his lesson?

No, not a bit of it! Whitey's career of evil was not over yet. Oh no!

But make no mistake about it, Whitey definitely had it coming.

I have already told you that Whitey liked to eat out. I have also mentioned that my Mum had an account with the Co-Op. Well, in those days, so did almost everyone else. These were the days when the Co-Op was king. They seemed to me, thinking about it now, to take care of just about everything. Everything from your birth certificate to your funeral and all your personal requirements in between. This included what was, without any doubt at all, Whitey's favourite place. Yes, his best, er, *client,* you might say.

The Co-Op butcher.

Alf, the butcher in question and the man at the heart of all this, told me all the stories about Whitey after his retirement when I met him and had a pint with him at the local club (by the way, the clubs were also king at this time as well as the Co-Op, but that's nothing to worry about. It's not as if they were ever in competition or anything). Whitey clearly relished his meal at the butcher's. After several visits to the neighbours for what amounted by comparison to no more than a starter course, he would be running so fast that he would sometimes topple over as he negotiated the hairpin bend into the shop's entrance. This was Whitey's personal version of Xanadu. Here he would be fed scrap after scrap of all manner of meat and offal and stuffing until even Whitey's seemingly never-ending appetite was satisfied. And after this experience of doggy ecstasy, do you think Whitey's evil manners would have at least slowed down?

Wrong again!

There is something that I have not told you about Whitey, perhaps out of a sense of personal shyness. You see, Whitey's savagery with regard to food paled into insignificance by comparison to his appetite for sex. Yes, that's right. Whitey would not only sniff out the neighbours for pickings in terms of food. He sired every bitch he could find. No matter what the breed, or the size, nothing proved even vaguely challenging for him. It didn't take long until there were many dogs in our village with an all too striking resemblance to the lad.

Yes, Whitey was sex-mad! But his day of doom was fast approaching. And for that, we must return to Alf's world.

The business conducted over the counter of the village's butcher shop was normally done at a fairly gradual, and quite stately, but constant pace. People would come into Alf's premises either one or two at a time. In those days, no one would bulk-buy. There were fridges in people's homes, yes, but these were very small, powered by gas, and it's hard to imagine now, but not everyone had one. Alf had a huge cold-room at the back of the shop, just inside to the left of the delivery bay. He told me once that he was always glad that that was its location, because on the days when he did relief work at other branches, he found himself exhausted there, not because of the hard work, but because the cold-rooms in these other premises took up half of the front end of the shop, and the boys on the van would only ever come as far as the loading bay which was at the back. He shrugged indifferently as he spoke of this in retrospect, because, although he was mildly annoyed with the situation, he knew that they had their job to do and he had his, and as far as they were concerned, they were under no obligation to him whatsoever, even though they all had the same boss.

But none of that was the case at his *home* shop, our village shop. On that particular day, as he put it, the heavy stone door of the cold-room had been left slightly ajar, because, unusually, and especially as it was mid-week, the shop was very busy and Alf was reduced to hurrying in and out of the cold-room in order to get supplies to serve his customers. In the middle of this fairly rare experience, in comes Whitey, racing through the entrance at virtually suicidal speed in dog terms, only having to slam on the brakes due to the presence of more people in the shop than usual. I say slam on the brakes as a figure of speech, because, as you obviously know, Whitey, like all dogs, did not actually have brakes. But to his credit, he tried his best. Unfortunately, his best was a terrible failure, knocking people over like skittles as he rolled in like an oversized canine bowling ball. Everyone started shouting and getting upset, including, of course, poor old Alf. He rushed around his counter to where everyone was, and very hurriedly helped the fallen to their feet. In the middle of all this confusion, Whitey, of course, had been forgotten. But you see, like all true bullies, Whitey in the end must have been a coward, and, in the ensuing chaos, scrambled for the nearest refuge in a state of what must have been for him sheer terror. Refuge in this case, yes, taking the form of Alf's cold-room. Just like his actions at our garden shed, he scrambled inside. Eventually, the situation calmed down and with everyone back on their feet, clothing straightened and dignity restored, they thanked Alf, who made sure they all still had their respective purchases. He also gave them each a small packet of minced beef as an act of compensation for their ordeal before they left. As an encouragement to come back again. It must be said that people *were* different then.

But Whitey's whereabouts remained a total mystery. Not that Alf's thoughts on the matter were so preoccupied as that. He looked around and about, this way and that, and, finding neither sight nor sign, nor for that matter sound, or any other such evidence of Whitey's presence, closed tight the cold-room door, securing it for the night with a huge padlock. Then, looking at the shop clock, it was half past four. This was something he remembered clearly when he told the police; that being almost closing time, he busied himself with the paper-roll and covered the remaining shop-front stock in the display counters, swept the floor and left for the night, unknowingly leaving Whitey sealed up in short-lived heaven. It didn't matter that it was pitch-black, or that it was freezing cold. I don't know if dogs can see in the dark like cats can, but Whitey helped himself to as much as he could reach. But as the cold and the dark began to kick in, Whitey was at last reduced to a scared animal, and started scratching at the door. But scratch as he may, the door of Alf's cold-room was made of solid stone, eighteen inches thick and probably bomb-proof for all I know. There was no way out for old Whitey.

Old Whitey was buried alive! You might say...

As I have already said, Whitey's presence in the village

was not only tolerated, but for reasons still to this day unknown to me, loved. I repeat this, because on the night of Whitey's absence from the village, my Mum, yes my Mum! not my father, decided to take matters into her own hands. What was her decision? Well, she organised what amounted to a search party to go out looking for him. This search party, you must understand, only consisted of my Mum, my father and me, Hawkey expressing the opinion that he was merely tagging along against his better judgement, being soundly convinced that the lad was quite safe and capable of looking after himself and finding his way home as and when he saw fit. An opinion with which I heartily agreed. Our next-door neighbours either side came too. Because, they said, ah, pity for him. And to be fair, we left no stone unturned. We knocked doors, looked up the woods and down the lake. My father even went up to see if he was in the kennels, but there was no Whitey to be seen anywhere. And with being locked in the cold-room, even if he was squealing, we couldn't hear him, either. In the end, common sense prevailed, and we all went home.

Then dawned the morning after.

As you may rightly assume, it was poor old Alf's lot to open the door to poor old Whitey after his night in cold storage. And what do you think? That poor old Whitey had frozen to a solid block of ice?

No such luck!

Alf was a big, well-fed, rugby-playing Welshman, but as soon as he opened his shop's cold-room door, he was attacked at high velocity and knocked to the floor by a huge white dog smeared with blood. Alf said he looked as if he had been fighting in the pit. Convinced he was about to be badly bitten, with his huge right arm managed in a split-second to land a solid punch right squarely on the dog's jaw, sending him skidding across the shop floor. With energy fuelled by pure adrenaline, Alf was back on his feet and ran to the dog and kicked him out into the street. The right-footed kick that had been so effective in scoring so many conversions on the rugby field on Saturday afternoons after the shop was closed, sent Whitey skidding over the road, where he ran home squealing in pain and sounding more like a pig than a dog.

It was the squeal of pain heard by the whole village.

You know by now that Whitey was a fast runner, but this time he broke all records. He bounded down the main road like a bolt of lightning. It was just as well our front door was open at the time, because I reckon that if it had been closed, Whitey would have smashed through it as if it was matchwood by the sheer force of his speed. He tore through our living room, through the kitchen and out up the garden into the shed, where I think he would have been wise to spend the rest of his days.

If these events had happened today, Whitey would definitely have been destroyed. And, to be fair, as he had done serious damage to Alf's shop and stock, Alf was right to ban not only Whitey, but all dogs from then on. But when the police, who turned up at the Co-Op manager's request, asked him if he wanted to press charges, Alf very charitably declined; partly out of genuine neighbourliness, and partly out of admitting his share of responsibility, because he knew that the dog had come into the shop, but Alf had failed to make sure that he was gone. Alf and my father agreed to pay half each for the loss of the meat in the cold-room. But it was a pretty scary experience for Alf, all the same.

As for Whitey, what was to become of him?

Whitey's story ends, in fact, very sadly. He stayed in the shed for a couple of days. Eventually, my father took pity on him and brought him into the kitchen and dressed his wounds. He was clearly very shaken by the whole thing, and it is true to say that he was never the same.

But the reformed Whitey didn't last long.

The main road of our village even to this day has a nasty bend with a blind spot about two hundred yards from our house up towards Alf's Co-Op butcher's shop. We don't know if Whitey was timidly venturing back there in search of another banquet, or in walking slowly as an act of doggy penitence, but a Post Office van hit him and the poor thing had to be put down.

Believe it or not, in spite of everything I have said about old Whitey, when I came home from school that day, I found my Mum crying. When she told me what had happened, I cried too. Even now, I get a pang when I think of him. I think now, perhaps Whitey was an animal version of the village idiot, or the village character, or something. Whatever he was, I have to admit that my father was right; it *was* good for a boy to have a dog and to learn through that and other ways, the virtue and pleasure of companionship.

But that whole world is gone now. There are no more dog fights, nor any blood sports for that matter. And there are no more tough guys like Hawkey, either. The clubs are no longer king, and neither is the Co-Op. People don't leave their doors open anymore, and life is a lot more complicated. I make no judgement about this – it's not like I'm saying it was better then than now. I'm just saying that it's, well, all gone now, and now we have something different.

A New World Dawns

It is a terrible thing to lose your parents, and when this happened I was totally devastated, as I'm sure you will understand. As I have already said and now say again, they were really great people and we had lots of fun together, and yes, old Whitey included. We never went on foreign holidays, but the more quaint variety, if you like. Things like coach day-trips, and caravan parks, where it always rained and we ended up playing cards in the "van", as my father insisted on calling it. But, the highlight for us was the holiday camps. I really still can't honestly remember whether or not I actually liked them at the time, because now their memory is coloured by the nostalgia of spending precious time with my parents, combined with the clichéd way those holidays, and for that matter, those times generally, are portrayed by the media nowadays. But my parents loved them. I guess the part that never goes away from me when I recall this is the completely disarming innocence of it all. So, as far as foreign travel and all that was concerned, neither of my parents was interested. Besides, America was too far away, and as for Europe, well, the Second World War was too fresh a memory for people of my parents' generation to have any objective opinions about *that*, thank you very much. I always dreamed about going to America because of the comics. Call me stupid if you like, but I actually believed that there really were such things as superheroes and that they all lived in America. Come on! Make some allowances – I was only a child, for goodness sake! I always thought that it would be very exciting to go there and meet them. Believe it or not, my Dad didn't like me reading American comics. He thought that they were far too violent for children and urged me to read the British comics instead. This I did, but there was no cure for me. I would be a superhero fan!

The death of my father was terrible by any standards. Not only the fact that I lost him at the age of seventeen, but seeing him become so ill and incapable of moving or speaking, and being like that for about a year, getting gradually worse and worse every day. My Mum cared for him night and day without stopping. This clearly took too much out of her, and about two and a half years later she passed away too. My father was the only man she had ever even as much as fancied. My Mum had a childhood friend called Jan, and when they were teenagers, they made a bet with each other to see who would get married first. Jan always told my Mum that she had boyfriend after boyfriend, but never invited my Mum to meet any of them. Eventually my Mum wondered if she was making them all up. But then, completely out of the blue, my Mum met Dennis, and, yes, she did invite Jan to meet him. Jan said that she was happy for my Mum, but my Mum thought she didn't mean it – she told me when it was just me and her that Jan was probably jealous. But still, they stayed friends. Jan seemed to get old before her time, and my Mum used to send me round her house to dig her garden and light her fire. Yes, this earned me a couple of shillings a week pocket money, but being there was such a depressing experience. You could almost taste the loneliness in the air. It was an atmosphere of permanent bereavement. Jan passed away very suddenly. No, she didn't have a heart attack or anything like that. Come to think about it, I don't really know what she died of, but it was only my Mum and me that went to her funeral. Then, after that, my Mum was gone too. My parents were truly beautiful people. I know this is my biography, but I'm sorely tempted at this point to make it theirs right now. My father's war record, and the issue about medals. The way he met my Mum, and why they decided to move to Wales.

But the truth is, you are reading this because you want to know about me. Not them. I never expected to make it big, even though I did. All I wanted to do was get by. Not necessarily to get rich, but to be comfortable, as the saying goes. Even my planning the whole thing felt like I was going through the motions because I was being driven by someone else. But when that happened, and it became the enormous success that it was, my first thought was, what would my parents think of me? I honestly believe they would have been proud of me.

I never went to university. That was for the Grammar School boys. I would be Secondary Modern! There was too much inverted snobbery in my father for that to happen! After my Mum passed away, I had a job riding a bike for a local private butcher, making deliveries. Alf had retired, and competition was slowly starting to come in, even in the early seventies, and so the Co-Op, though it was still a force to be reckoned with, was not the only butcher in town anymore. As I keep saying, my parents were excellent people, and as well as providing for me throughout the whole of their lives, my father paid cash for our house, thus making sure I would always be secure with a roof over my head. So there were never any worries about security or anything like that. I had several girlfriends, one of whom I did introduce to my mother, but had not really gone steady with any of them, as such. And to tell you the truth, I didn't see much future in delivering meat as a career. It would have been different if there was a chance of getting promoted to shop work, but after a year and a half, it was pretty obvious to me that this was something that was just not going to happen. My father always reckoned that if you want to know if you should do something or not, a good thing to do is imagine that you are old and look back on what you are thinking about doing and imagine that you have done it for years and are now retired from it. Sit comfortably and ask yourself, do you regret it or are you glad you did it? With that thought in mind, it seemed right to me that a fresh course of action was needed. But what? I thought about trying to find work in another town. But then, as if hit by a bolt of lightning, I thought, what about not only a different town, but a whole different country!

But which one?

Well, for no better reason than that it was the nearest, I chose France. Today, you would call me a backpacker, but not then. As far as I was concerned at the time, I simply called the whole thing a working holiday. Nothing sophisticated or complicated about it. Considering the alternatives, though, you could argue the case for simply looking for another job, and not for leaving the country! Well, in fact, I did look for another job, several jobs in fact. Granted, the employment market was a different world to that of today. True, there was plenty of work about, and I was very much looking forward to doing some of it! In those days, in business, if you had only the vaguest of ideas about what you wanted to do, it was totally doable and you had every right to expect it to succeed. But that was just it. My father had found something he loved doing, namely breeding dogs. And to be fair, he made a good living at it. It was on the strength of this that he bought the house that I was actually born in and made it the permanent family home, and he did it without a mortgage or anything. Yes, he paid cash for it! Try doing that today! It wasn't very big, but on the day that he was handed the front door key, he said that you could hardly hold him down. Just imagine the pride! And most importantly, he had found that vital key thing he most loved doing in the world by being around people and finding something that needed to be done and learning very quickly what was needed to do it, and how to do it well. He used to say that he had taken to breeding dogs almost by accident.

And that is the way I see it. I did my best to put that house in mothballs before I left, packed a duffel bag and made my way to the nearest cross-Channel ferry. I was definitely France bound! I was convinced that I would find something for myself in the same way that Hawkey did. But not something involving bloodsports!

Obviously.

My French Adventure

It was in a high-spirited frame of mind and thorough-going appetite for life that I crossed the English Channel, my parents' views on that subject notwithstanding. I felt that I knew, just absolutely certainly knew, that somewhere out there, whether it be in France or anywhere else for that matter, that somewhere, anywhere, I would find something I was good at. Just like my father. Well, it had to be worth a try, at least, hey?

But let's try to keep both my feet on the ground for the moment. You see, for me at that time, any lavish travel was out. I was absolutely not a first class passenger! I was determined to do this, which, even before I left, still seemed totally crazy in spite of having decided to do it. I knew that not only was I going to have to travel light, but I was going to have to choose the cheapest possible way of transport and accommodation.

To put it simply, I would have to walk and sleep outside.

This walking, I assumed, would of course mean a *lot* of walking. Probably a great deal more walking than I was used to doing, even though I was still in my twenties. And sleeping out of doors, of course, would mean trying to find something to keep myself warm. And I didn't even own a sleeping bag! Oh dear, perhaps I wasn't ready for all this...

Wrong! I was completely speechless with amazement when I arrived. I had never left British soil, so I was completely unprepared for what I was about to see. It was a scene of unabridged beauty. I had got off the ferry and even though my first and most important thought was to find a part-time job to pay my way, all the worries that I had nursed at sea seemed to fade away. The ferry harbour was impressive in its way, being well thought out and pleasant. Everyone there was friendly, helpful and efficient. One of the port officials spoke English and directed me to a local coastal village, which was not too far, called Argent Port de Bluff, where, he assured me, I would find a friendly welcome. It was very rural, once I got away from the busy harbour complex, with golden fields stretching upwards away into the distance to my left, and the blue sea descending to my right.

I thought I was in a film or something!

Now if you're waiting for a black moment to arrive, where, in spite of being so happy in this scene of such beauty, something goes horribly and tragically wrong, forget about it. I was too happy to entertain any morbid contemplations of any variety - even for a minute. In coming here, I had not laid out anything like a definite plan of action, or a strategy, or whatever else you want to call it. And do you know what? It seemed to me that this was the sort of place where that frame of mind was right at home! Argent Port de Bluff was the sort of place where no one ever made a plan about anything. It was quaint and old-fashioned, brightly coloured with every sort of shop you can think of recreated in miniature. Then there were the smells; they came from everywhere! Every kind of food you can imagine! And yet for me the strange thing was that no one, and I repeat this, no one was ever in a hurry! How they managed that was a total mystery to me. It was non-functional on many things, with very little by way of mod cons. But that was what made it wonderful. Well, to me at least. Everyone was very pleasant and relaxed, and within what must have been only an hour of arriving there I was made as welcome as if I was a valued comrade returning after being away too long, served a nice meal of a fish dinner, with a very sweet cake afterwards, then washed down with some white wine, and then before I knew it, was offered a room and small job sweeping floors and carrying out meals in four, yes four! of the local cafés, thus providing for myself a small wage in what was a dreamy, beautiful place. What more could anyone ask?

You have probably guessed that I fell in love with the place pretty much straight away. Honestly, there was absolutely nothing not to like. The colours and beauty of the place, together with the quaintness of the little buildings, combined to create a scenery and atmosphere that was truly breathtaking, the smells of all the different foods, the friendly local people, with their happy, relaxed approach to life, all combined to make me feel as if I was in a different world.

Which of course I was.

The language barrier was definitely going to be one of the main problems I would face, if not *the* problem. But not even that was the case. In fact, quite the reverse. Although I considered myself no language expert by any means, I picked it up very quickly. This was a real surprise even to me, but it was because, although the people were provincial and local, and understood very little English, they found a way to use the barrier to get to know me. They would explain little words that hold the sentences together and throw in the odd test about children and childhood and family and such, and slowly we would communicate in a very quaint and beautiful way. Amazing! All this helped enormously, not only with my job, but of course to thoroughly enjoy my time there. I guess for most people, it would be the kind of place that, once they find it, they would stay there for the rest of their lives. My life in Argent Port de Bluff was ideal. I spent my time slowly sweeping floors, chatting with the customers, eating without putting on any weight, and walking around the village on errands for various people who always rewarded me with more of their beautiful food, wine and pleasant chat. It is a safe guess that within the first month, I felt like I had been there all my life.

And yes, there was even a romantic flirtation to be had!

Her name was Vientianne Marchand and she was sweetness personified. Aged only twenty-three, short, very petite, with close-cut jet black hair that even so managed to curl prettily at the edges, she epitomised all things French. But she was not local to the village. She had moved here from more sophisticated, southerly climes. Like me, she was searching for a new chapter in her life. Also, like me, she had settled here because she liked the pace of life and took a low-paying job to at least feed herself. At first, all we seemed to do was smile at each other when we passed, either in the village or in the café where she worked, and laughed too much when either of us got something wrong. The older villagers sat lazily in the shade and watched us and smiled at each other. They knew there was romance in the air!

Vientianne, or Vivvy, as she liked to be called, had studied journalism and the arts at the Université Golden Sierra pour les filles at Vale Côté Eau, and it could be argued, she said, that she was wasted here, as a maid in a café, but that was the way she liked it. She said that there was a lot of stress at Vale and that because she had wanted to write to spread beauty and beautiful thoughts all around to the people she knew and the wider public, too, if they would have her, it came as a great and unpleasant surprise to her that there was stress and negativity all around her and she felt that she was not being allowed to express herself. Together with this was the calamity of always being under someone else's schedule, and this made her angry and cynical. This situation here was for her, the perfect solution. It was a beautiful place, and she could talk about pleasant things with people who were at ease and consequently learn many things. And since she was aware of what would have been expected of her at Vale, and knowing that no one here would be able to make those kinds of demands on her ever again, she decided in her spare time to redouble her efforts in her studies, and in the outcome produce much more. Eventually, some local and some less regional editors were very impressed with her work and some of it was bought by them. This, of course, pleased her very much, but she was a little sad with herself because she said that she could feel the presence of anger inside her; anger put there by Vale. She said that she no longer felt beautiful.

Nothing could have been further from the truth, and I wasted no time in telling her that.

She gave me a lot of her work, but I have to confess that I

did not keep much of it. But I did keep some, and as I think of her sadness now, a sadness that made her even more beautiful, in my opinion, I am going to include my favourite poem of hers. It was called "Cri d'Amour", or "Love's Cry".

Le sourire sur ton visage quand tu éclates avec plaisir,
Le frisson de l'etreinte
dans le soleil de l'après-midi. Ton arôme et ton sourire Ils me
remplissent extase Où le rire est terminé
et l'amour se fait.
Un cri du coeur
où le monde se lasse.
Lors de désintégrations de beauté et de l'innocence meurt;
Quand mon âme veut planer et crier avec actions de grâces
laissez la beauté de la verité éclipser les mensonges.

English translation (mine):

The smile on your face
when you burst out with pleasure, The thrill of embrace
In the afternoon sun; Your smell and your smile they fill me
with ecstasy when laughter is finished and loving is done.
A cry of the heart
when the world grows tired, when beauty decays
and innocence dies;
when my soul wants to soar and cry out with thanksgiving, let
the beauty of truth overshadow the lies.

I enjoyed being in her company. And I can honestly admit that she opened my eyes to a lot of unexpected experiences in a lot of unexpected ways. In all my life up to this point, poetry, music, art and the like had been something that was strictly in the background. It's not that I did not like it, but it was something either I saw or heard and then passed by, or something I was polite about with someone else because I knew they liked it. It was definitely not something that took up much of my personal time or interest. I remember that my father liked Country and Western music, but he would never go as far as to actually buy a record. I remember once, when he did an odd job for a neighbour, his payment was a heavy vinyl boxed set of Wagner's Symphonies. I was never to know his opinions about Wagner's music, but they could not have amounted to very much because the records were never played. But I liked the picture on the box, though, because it had dragons on it. And being from Wales and all! But again that was as far as it went.

But with Vivvy it was totally different. Her room was full of music, with a record player and lots of records. Also, she could tell me the story of each artist or group, and would wax very eloquent on her opinions about everything each one of them did. I have obviously thought about her a lot, and I think sadly that ultimately her attempt to escape from Vale was a failure. You see, the thing is, she came to Argent Port de Bluff to get away from the chaos and stress put on her at Vale. Yet all she managed to do in the end was to bring that same stress and chaos with her. I think before she started at Vale, she must have been a very sweet little girl, always smiling and laughing. But then, when discipline set in, and time for hard work came, well, she simply wasn't prepared for it. And in spite of all the pleasantness she showed to everyone around her, including me, the damage had already been done.

But I was not aware of any of that at the time.

Her frustration came out in the music she liked best.

Heavy rock. Very unusual for a girl, I thought. Perhaps now you're starting to fit a piece or two together. It was the mid-seventies and the old clean-cut styles and hippie styles of the sixties were changing and Glam Rock and Heavy Metal was evolving. My first reaction to it all was along the lines, you might say, of "what the [BLEEP] is that!", but Vivvy said that I was being a prig. I must have appeared very simple-minded to her when I said that. I had no idea then what a prig was, but it definitely didn't sound good. She just laughed and played it again. It's very strange, you know, the effect that repetition, a lot of wine and a beautiful French girlfriend can have! By the time she had finished, I liked it! At first, I hated it, but she poured me another glass of wine and played me some more. Then I said that it was a mad version of the sixties protest songs, but with those, you could tell what they were protesting about, but you had no idea with this lot! Her reply to this was very simple. Yes, she poured me yet another glass of wine and played some more.

"Okay!" I eventually asked, "just tell me who this is, then."

When she answered, I just burst out laughing. It was a band, and I'm never likely to forget this, called Johnny Dollz. I couldn't help it; they were hysterical. I think I hurt myself by laughing so much. I said that they looked like something out of a pantomime, dressed like girls and everything. She was confused, not having any idea what a pantomime was, and the more I tried to explain, the more confused *she* got. I just didn't see that one coming. I think I managed to explain that a pantomime was a show my parents took me to see when I was a child. She was annoyed at my remarks, and, yes, poured me another glass of wine and played some more. This went on for I don't remember how long until she said that she was going to bed. Good night. She seemed annoyed. She was convinced that she had failed to persuade me. And, truth be told, although it was a pleasant evening, the whole thing had struck me as completely silly. But you know how it is, I didn't want to offend her, so the following morning I wore a red headband and played air-guitar every time I passed her. To my great delight, she smiled ever so sweetly, we kissed and everyone laughed and applauded. Was the upshot of this that I found it easy to listen to and relate to? I'll be honest. It was really all because of her!

And it was far more successful than I could possibly have bargained for. The very next day after my evening of musical metamorphosis, and my public declaration of it, we moved in together. We decided that we would share everything together and that there would be no secrets, no, none at all.

The next three months were what can only be described as heaven on earth. We went the full distance as far as dreamy romances are concerned. You know, doing literally everything together – and yes, I do, of course, mean everything. Going everywhere together. Every moment when we were apart being nothing other than painful, both physically and mentally, this only serving to make our time together even more intense. I told her my whole story up to that point, and she greeted my every word as if it were a revelation, wide-eyed with amazement. She looked oh so achingly adorable and cute as she listened to me, her almost worshipful facial expression would just inspire me to keep on talking.

And then the axis would shift, eventually making it her turn to do some talking. And I seriously have to tell you that when she started to talk, it was something else. She was very educated and effortlessly eloquent, having a way with words that was far superior to mine.

And I foolishly convinced myself that it would last forever.

It was roughly three months later, on one of Argent Port de Bluff's normal beautiful sunny days that gave the impression of seamlessly melting into each other, that I first met Bernard Cahun. I was living in a beautiful place, where talking to people was very easy. They visited for all types of reason and they were, of course, all types of people, but Argent Port de Bluff had that sweet way of working its magic on its visitors so that, however stressed and irritable they were when they arrived, they soon relaxed and smiled and became willing to talk and open up in conversation. It was the couples that I most easily gravitated to, but it was only right to acknowledge the solitary traveller. Bernard was one such solitary man, but not overtly so. He was pleasant and polite, and easily engaged in conversation, not only with myself, but with his many other fellow visitors who had come to a place that every day felt more and more like home. My first conversation with him was what I had come to consider to be the normal one. That is, he did as everyone else did, by smiling and waving his hands in every direction and praising the beauty of the village. In subsequent chats he divulged that he was French, but confessed that, even though he had visited many places in the world, he had never really seen his own native land, and was now taking time out to do so. And inevitably, he guessed, was finding out many unknown things, not only about France, but about himself also; although he was slow to tell me precisely what his discoveries were, interior or exterior. He was also very surprised when I told him that I was not French. By the time we met, I had become fluent, my accent was local to the village and I had developed the easy, relaxed manner that was characteristic of the area. So it was very understandable that he would not think other than that I was as French as he. I admitted to him that I was flattered that he should think this of me. We were very relaxed in each other's company and neither of us ventured our opinions about any matters of controversy or convention, and we just got on with our own lives – he to his visit, and I to my work in the day, and on my time off, to Vivvy, who was at this time, everything to me.

It was not until he had extended his visit to three weeks, that I began to entertain the idea in my mind that Bernard Cahun had more protracted plans. My considered impression of him was that he was an intelligent, thoughtful man, capable of planning against every eventuality. Yet his true nature was more involved even than that. He said that it was undesirable to walk through life in a carefree way, and that this was never going to be the way he lived his life, nor ever had been. I found this very surprising, especially when I considered his general manner.

It was when he told me his full name. I mention this

because it was an important moment. Everything changed. For one thing, names in this place were relatively unimportant; the only real use for them being for that of business information like national and local tax. But in normal parlance, names served no more real purpose than "hey you", and full names were never used, and this was with regard to local people, let alone with visitors, whose names were hardly ever known, and never the full name.

I can remember it so clearly. I had been milling about with working, and chatting happily with customers, and as usual, although life was very busy, it is managed with a mixture of calm, ease and, yes, delight – this being drawn out of each person by the area itself, or so it seemed. I was wearing my normal white shirt, black bow tie, black waistcoat, black trousers and black boots. These were not pressed and polished to perfection. I was always in a crumpled state. Everyone seemed to like this. It was a motif, both of ruffled refinement, and being busy and friendly. I think I must have had a dozen things on my mind, both of what I had done and what I had left to do, besides all the things that I would suddenly and spontaneously be asked to do without warning. This was, I think, one such moment that epitomised for me the unexpected thing.

He was a well-built man of dark colouring, in his late twenties, but with a much older mind. As the time of his visit had lengthened, he became more scruffily dressed. There had clearly been a grooming in his past. I could also see that his coffee cup was empty, and picked up a jug from the nearest stove and filled it. He drank it quickly so that the cup was empty. I filled the cup again. Silently, he smiled and stooped his head to show his gratitude. I smiled and nodded back to show that I understood both his gesture and that I appreciated that morning's choice of level of communication, not wishing to press further. Then he reached out and touched my forearm, this having the effect of stopping my exit from his presence.

"Good morning, Mark." he said. I was astonished. He spoke in English. "My full name is Bernard Cahun." This was pronounced Kar- Hoon.

"Thank you," I replied, also in English, under his spell. "My name is Mark Bashford."

"I already knew that, as I am sure you are aware. Well, *Mark*," he said, his smile still holding, and still in English, "in that case, I would like to order two coffees, please."

"*Oui bien sûr, monsieur. Certainement,*" I replied, and, somewhat mildly annoyed, disappeared again to fetch a tray of fresh cups, saucers and spoons from just inside the door of my café. As I upturned them at his table, I silently puzzled over the identity of his mystery guest.

"The second coffee is for you," he said, as if reading my thoughts. He had respectfully returned to French after my somewhat clipped response to his order placed in English. It was obvious that all my attempts at keeping my own counsel had failed miserably. "Please sit down here," he said, gesturing to the seat opposite him at the table. "Surely you will do this, as everyone here is very apt to chat, including you."

I silently poured both coffees and obediently took my seat, resting the jug on a spare placemat at the table. He raised his cup and commenced our conversation by proposing a toast.

"To great success in business and in life!" he said, with his smile undiminished. I saw no harm in this. In fact, I quite agreed. I raised my cup to meet his, and we tapped cups together.

"To great success, wherever it can be found!" I replied warmly. We both laughed, and drank our coffees.

"You are very easy company, Mark. I observe in my time here that everyone responds well and pleasantly to you, and that you clearly enjoy your work here. I conclude that you are very good at your work for this reason."

I pursed my lips thoughtfully for a second, and answered, "I'm a waiter," and shrugged my shoulders. I was dumbfounded that he should even say such a thing. It was so obvious.

"But not just a waiter," he replied. "A really good waiter. Look at you. You work for four cafés all next to each other, and in the same village."

"Maybe so, but that is the way it is in this village. Everyone co-operates. No one competes. We all like each other, and I like it here. Sure, it's very hard work, but that doesn't matter. We enjoy life." I remember that I came to this conclusion the moment I had arrived at Argent Port De Bluff. Then he said it:

"Mark, what if I told you that I could make you rich." I noticed that at the moment he said that, his smile thinned ever so slightly. I shrugged my shoulders again.

"As a waiter? How? And why me?"

"Pour us both another coffee and I'll tell you." He laughed. I obliged. He was paying. "I understand that you don't make much money, and I also get it that you're happy with that. And to be very truthful with you, I totally respect that. Many people crave contentment – the very contentment you have now is what perhaps most people do not have, and if you want to walk away from me at this very moment, that is totally your own choice. Give me my bill, I will pay and leave right now." He paused for effect. I did not move, of course. "Okay. So here's the thing. You may not think you can be rich by being a waiter, but that is exactly where you are wrong! Tell me how much money do you think that the four cafés here make from all your hard work? Please don't misunderstand me, here. I'm not saying that they are doing anything wrong, or anything at all like that. What I am saying to you right here and now is that if you were the owner of these four cafés, it is you who would be rich, not them. And the most important thing is, I can show you how!"

"But all four café owners combined are not rich," I stammered.

He made no reply. I felt as if I was drowning. True, I loved it here, but his words, in spite of my remark, seemed to light a fire in my belly that I could not ignore. Suddenly, I was not happy.

"Okay, how?"

Vivvy's Crisis

Vivvy had a cousin, whose name was Sonia. Vivvy and Sonia had grown up as sisters because Sonia had never known her parents. She could never have known her father, because he had left as soon as he knew that Sonia's mother was pregnant. Her mother, Margot, Vivvy's aunt, sadly died in childbirth. Both Vivvy and Sonia were born only a matter of weeks apart. So, without hesitation, Vivvy's mother adopted the orphaned baby as her own and the child was christened Sonia. Vivvy's family gave Sonia a loving and happy home, full of laughter and sweet memories, but it was not to last.

Sonia came with family rebellion built-in.

This fledgling rebellion amounted to no more than a few childlike tantrums at first, but in spite of constantly being corrected, they became more frequent and severe. Sonia would scream loudly and madly at all the family's attempts to exercise patient and loving care and concern. It was always Vivvy's mother's wish to treat Sonia as her own. But Sonia's behaviour became more and more challenging.

As children, they shared the same bedroom, because Vivvy's mother held to the idea that children should be together. It was at night that Sonia would keep Vivvy awake by making strange and frightening noises. Many times, Vivvy tried to tell her mother that she was frightened and at first she, of course, was not believed. Then the bed-wetting started. But when this progressed to self-harming, they were separated. Everyone feared that Vivvy would be attacked during the night, which now appeared a distinct possibility. Also, the fact remained that such a sight as self-harming was upsetting for an *adult*, let alone a young child. Vivvy was a gentle child, who wanted to love everyone. But it seemed that Sonia simply did not want to be loved. Her reaction to being kept apart from Vivvy at night was to go into a demented rage, throwing things about and making a terrible fuss. For a few days, as all this continued, her parents came to the sad conclusion that they were losing control of her. But they persevered, watching her constantly and fretfully. But as Sonia grew worse, she refused food and began to waste away. Together with this, she resorted to violence. Eventually, Sonia was not allowed to pick up as much as a pencil, let alone a pair of scissors.

Then one day, Sonia told her already much-maligned family that she had become a witch! Their first response to this was to smile indulgently and, in spite of the experience of her previous episodes, to dismiss it all as just a silly phase. They were not in denial. Indeed, they were fully aware of how her mind had declined, but to be fair to them, they were by no means intolerant. But Sonia progressed to hallucinogenic drugs, holding tarot card readings to predict people's future and talking to the dead via a Ouija board, sometimes practising this alone. The family's patience had been in no small measure motivated by consideration for her tender age, that of sixteen. They were by now well aware that something had to be done before she reached the age of consent. They had tolerated and suffered from her deeply challenging behaviour for a long time.

But it was when they made the highly upsetting discovery that her drug habit had led to prostitution, which then furthered her occult behaviour, worsening her decline, that they decided to take the action of having her committed to a home for the mentally ill. This was done with the deepest sorrow, but with the honesty of knowing that she was beyond their power. They visited her regularly, but she would rage and shout and send them away. They always left her feeling upset and dismayed, and not a little guilty. Yet in spite even of all this, they refused to dismiss her as devil-possessed; choosing, as we would say today, to *be there* for her.

Vivvy had never told me anything of this, because she considered it too personal, and also because Sonia's life was now happening elsewhere. Her mother, in taking this measure, looked upon it as a way of guarding her. In fact, a way of guarding all the family. Perhaps it was her way of making up for the mistake of not believing her daughter at the beginning. Besides which, she did not want to bother me with it, and so well organised and established were her thoughts on the subject that it had never even come up in conversation. Her eventually telling me all about it was a very big step for her. Especially for me, perfect timing as it was, the day I wanted to tell her about Bernard's proposal. I was seriously floundering. As a result of my conversation with Bernard, I was a lot less happy than I had been. But this was completely unexpected. I felt frustrated, so all I could do now was to put completely aside everything I wanted to tell her.

And why was it so important to be telling me this story?

"Because I have had a telegram from my mother this

morning telling me Sonia is on her way here! I am sorry, but we have to leave right away!"

"But wait a minute," I protested. "You can't just run from her. You have to stand up against her. And if that is not possible, then we have to call the police!"

"No, no, no!" she shouted, shaking her head franticly as if to clear the very thought from her. "You don't understand! Sonia is now aged twenty-three. She can be very nice. That is her strength. That is how she makes her money from prostitution, remember! And also, when the people came to examine her from the mental home, she was very nice to them, too. It was the marks where she had hurt herself that told them that she was lying. When she knew that they didn't believe her, she went crazy. I don't know what to do if she appears here!" I looked right and left, as if I would find a reply would be hanging on the walls somewhere. But there was none. The walls remained silent to me.

"Well, what do you think *she* will do?" I knew I was clutching at straws. "Does she even know where you are, the address, I mean?"

"Oh please! You know that that is not something she needs! We are both seen in and around the village every day! We are the two most obvious people here! The two young lovers! You have to trust me about this! I wish we could stay, but..."

"Wait a minute!" I shouted, suddenly bright again with inspiration, "Okay, we need to get away from her. But listen! Telegram your mother to call the police, and we will simply quickly go on holiday together! No one in the village is going to tell her about us, and we will be away, and the police will have returned her to the protection of the home and to custody by the time we return from holiday! Come on, Vivvy, it's a great idea, and we never have any time off! What do you say?" She was immediately quiet and I was relieved to see that she was at least appearing to think about it.

"Well..." she answered diminutively, making puppy eyes, "do you think we'll be allowed? To have the time off? It's the full summer and they need all the help they can get. If help were no problem, you would not be working in four cafés at once..." She began to cry, and that was the worst part for me then.

"All we can do is ask," I sighed. I sat down next to her on the bed that was the only seating in our tiny room, and cuddled her as tenderly as I could. It was awful seeing her this way. "All we can do is ask," I whispered to her again. I simply did not know what else to say.

Meanwhile, it felt like Bernard was standing outside, waiting for my answer. But I knew that I could not tell it to Vivvy! That was simply the worst thing possible. Anything else, no matter how small, I was afraid it would send her over the edge, and she was far too close to that for the entrance of more information than she could handle. I got up and ran franticly outside into the village square and looked around everyone in the crowd to see Robert, the owner of the main café. If I could find him and tell him, or if not him, tell any one of my colleagues, they would hopefully let Robert know. It was so annoying that I could not get past them, because they all wanted to chat and say the usual things, but that was simply not something I was capable of doing right then. Everything looked the same and sounded the same, with the same happy chatter, the same street musicians playing for coins and the fragrances of the meals being served. But it was as if I was in a different world to everyone else while at the same time being right there and then with them. If only Robert would appear and save me. Eventually, after repeatedly telling people that I could not take their order at the moment but that there was a waitress named Mimi who would be only too ready to take whatever they would like to order as soon as she was free, I managed to push my way through the main entrance to Robert's café. I knew that once I was inside the entrance, and if Robert was there, he would be easy to find, because the majority of customers were seated at the tables outside on the square. I was upset to find that Robert was not there, but then just as suddenly he rushed past me through the entrance and slammed an order chit on the spike so hard on the counter that I thought he had impaled his hand, but he had not. There was no time for relief. He shouted the order through the kitchen serving hatch to the chef with a loudness we both shared. At the sight of all this, I felt very sad. I was not feeling very hopeful for my request, almost wishing to myself that I could forget all about it. But I remembered the words that I had used to comfort Vivvy and took a deep breath.

"Oh, Mark! Mark! My dear boy!" Robert exclaimed. "I am so glad to see you! Just look at it out there!" giving both my shoulders a hard and friendly slap. To his great credit, as busy as he was, Robert was always friendly and smiled through everything. I sighed and took another deep breath.

"Vivvy and I have to go to Vale for a week, maybe two. I am so sorry, Robert, but it is for her an emergency." He rolled his eyes around in a thoughtful way for a couple of seconds.

"If you can finish today for me, please, you can go on Monday, but don't forget to tell Mimi as all your tips for that time off will be hers. It is the fair thing to do. Do you agree?" I had, of course, no objections to this and fully agreed to Robert's proposal as a good compromise. We kissed each other on both cheeks and got on with our respective tasks. I was now a little more hopeful that Vivvy was going to be very pleased.

Bernard had been for the whole of that day, unknown to me but still unsurprisingly, seated among the crowd on the square. At no time had he even once attempted to make himself known, though it was obvious that he would have seen me. He had a carefully cultivated persona, giving to all the impression of an intelligent man of leisure. He was, of course, all that, but a whole lot more. Let me at least, in all my hurry and confusion, credit him with that, I thought. So, even though I was fully engaged with work, my mind for the rest of the day was not on the square, because for all its happy chaos, which I normally adored and in a real sense still miss very much, it seemed very far away, and I was very sad about that. My most urgent preoccupation was Vivvy.

But eventually, I found Bernard. By this time, the time when it came, I did not actually want to find Bernard at all. I was too worried about Vivvy, and I could not find Mimi and time was running out. There were simply too many thoughts in my head to deal with him. But Bernard was not alone. I was somewhat relieved about this. I guessed that it would be easier to greet them both. Then, if necessary, take their order and escape. And escape was the way I felt about it. Bernard had taken away from me my contentment with a lovely place, and this was now compounded by my worry for Vivvy. I presumed that the woman was a friend of his, probably an intimate friend, judging by the way she was dressed and the way she was sat, leaning forward in a low-cut yellow flower-print summer dress. She was clearly seducing him. I paid little attention to this, as it happened constantly. But I could not avoid him because I found myself approaching his table head-on, as it were. We fell into each other's stare.

"Ah! Mark!" he cried out. If you wanted to be heard in this crowd, you had to make a noise. "So good to see you at last! I would ask you to join us, but you can see how it is today, heh! But I must ask according to my nature if you have considered my offer. We both know that it is a good one, but I understand that you have to ask your beautiful girlfriend if she would like to climb on board with us! That I, of course, understand fully." He was smiling the whole time he was saying this. I guessed it was because of what he was anticipating with the woman, rather than anything I would be likely to say to him.

"Yes. That is very much the case." I smiled back awkwardly. "I will tell you very soon." Then, suddenly remembering: "Do you have an order, please?"

"Oh no. That is not necessary. The older gentleman has taken care of all that. *Pah!* How rude of me! I am so sorry, Mark!" He turned his gaze to the smiling woman's face and, looking into her piercing green eyes, took her hand. "I am sorry to you too, dear Sonia."

As Bernard turned his head to face me again, I can honestly say that I did not hear what he was saying and I knew it was not because of the noise of the crowd. I watched his lips move, but was simply not registering his words. My mind had gone blank, and I ran through the crowd. I pushed hard through them, using both outstretched hands paddling left and right as I went. The only thought in my mind at that point was: surely this could not be true. It must be a sheer coincidence that the girl was named Sonia, and it is obvious that there is more than one girl in the world with that name, even as I knew that there is more than one man in the world with my own name. And so, with the inside of my head feeling like so many scrambled eggs, I pushed on through the crowd until I got to the other side, which I hoped was close to our room, while at the same time hoping that Bernard and the woman he was with had not followed me. I looked back and all around, scanning as many faces as I could, thinking that if they were offended by my staring at them, so what. I was looking for Bernard. But I was hindered in this by being panicked and breathless and exhausted. I rested both my hands on my knees and stared down at the pavement. This was a beautiful place and I didn't want to leave it, but because of this crazy woman, both myself and the girlfriend of my dreams were being uprooted by fear. Also, I had promised Robert that I would finish the shift, but now I could not. Both Vivvy and I had to leave. I was so angry! I stood up straight again, and took a deep breath, scared that both Bernard and Sonia would be standing there right next to me, but thankfully they were not. Since being in France, I had seen many movies – more than I had ever seen at home, in fact – and suddenly I thought that I had seen too many, thinking like this. Again, though, I darted my stare this way and that, just to make sure. Then, convinced that they were nowhere near, I turned left instead of right at the square and took a longer route back to our room, just in case.

But to my horror, Vivvy was not there when I arrived. In a state of high panic, I searched in the drawers and cupboard, and my discoveries made things worse. With the notable exception of Vivvy's collection of record albums, neither of us had much by way of possessions, but all her things were gone, except these. There was no mess. Everything looked as organised as she always made sure it was. I had absolutely no idea what to do. I called out, but there was no answer. Where was she? What had she done? Did she plan to return to Vale without me and escape back home? Had she heard that Sonia was here in the village? As the questions crowded my mind, I realised that the last one was entirely possible. As far as I was concerned, the situation had now become entirely unmanageable. The best thing possible for us would have been that we stayed together, but now we were apart. I was suddenly angry with myself for asking Robert for permission to leave, because now that was completely irrelevant. Sonia had witnessed Bernard calling me by name and mentioning that I had a girlfriend. I quickly changed and put my few belongings into my old duffel bag, then took an agonising last look around the room, and left. More questions surfaced. What to do next? Where to go next? And where was Vivvy! It's so different now, but there were no mobile phones then. So all I could do was guess. I decided that it was most likely that she had made for the railway station. So I ran there as fast as I could. I had no idea of the times of the trains, if Vivvy *was* there, where she would be going, or what to do if she was not there.

But thankfully, oh so thankfully, my guesswork on this most vital situation, was correct. I cannot express the relief and joy I felt when I saw her there on the single platform of the tiny station. I could see that she had been crying, so I thought it best not to mention Sonia. We embraced for a long time, and stood together silently. Words were beyond us. It felt right then that we would simply go to wherever the next train was going. It really did not matter where to either of us.

A Major Steps In

We must have waited about thirty-five minutes before a train arrived. It may not sound a long time, but when you don't know *if* a train will arrive, *when* a train will arrive, or where it's going, it felt like we were there for days. The train that did finally arrive was going to a town called Ville De Reines, and thus, so were we. It was yet another of those things that we wordlessly decided together.

But when we got on board, we found to our frustration that many of the compartments were either full or reserved.

"Oh, that's it!" groaned Vivvy, in complete despair of finding a vacant compartment, let alone a vacant seat, and slid down tiredly to the floor under the corridor window, not remotely interested in the passing scenery. I looked nervously around. I knew Vivvy was not in any mood to listen to reason. Sonia's all too untimely presence in the village, which it was appearing very possible that Vivvy had known about, would have badly rattled her, and I decided that now was not the time to try to talk common sense to her, but I also knew that we needed to find a vacant compartment, and in one of them some unreserved seats.

At any moment now, because we had recently boarded, the conductor would be around to either inspect our tickets or collect our fares, and if he saw us in the passageway unseated here, he would be in no mood for any compromise or delicate talk. He would have his job to do and very soon he would be doing it. I had to think of something quickly.

I simply and silently took her by both her hands, stared and smiled at her directly in her face and drew her to her feet. She objected to this with her eyes, but co-operated with me, and as we continued along in this same dream-like manner, who should we meet in just a few seconds at the most, but the conductor walking toward us.

"Good afternoon, sir and miss," he said. He was not pleasant, but I could tell he was not in a bad mood. "Do you have tickets or do you want to buy them right now?"

"I would like to buy them of course, please." I smiled gently back. I knew what it was like to be on my feet all day and at the same time try to be pleasant. I guessed this was harder for him than it would have been for me. "One ticket each for the rest of the journey until its termination, thank you."

"This is the First Class Coach. Could you tell me where you are seated, please." he nodded courteously at my reply. At this I shrugged my shoulders.

"I'm so sorry, sir, but we can't find anywhere. The compartments are either full or reserved. It's a large train and I'm sure we'll find somewhere soon, but..." I repeated my shrugging. He pursed his lips in thought for a moment. Then he smiled, and as if agreeing with himself, he nodded his head.

"Yes. We are very busy today. This happens sometimes. There must be some special reason for it. I don't know what it is. But I may have a solution for you both. Come with me, please." Then he walked away from us in the opposite direction of his approach. We obeyed, with Vivvy in front, me behind and the conductor leading the way. He stared into each compartment as he went, until eventually he stopped at one. Suddenly his face changed. He grinned widely at its single occupant, and knocked sharply on the glass.

"Wake up, Major!" he shouted, jovially. "At your best! You have guests!" He turned to us, still grinning, without waiting for a reply. "Please be introduced to Major Benoît Allais. He speaks very loudly, but do not be afraid of him. He travels regularly, so I don't mind interrupting him every once in a while. Also, we are friends, so don't worry." By now, the conductor looked quite mischievous.

The compartment's single, aged, portly, sleeping, plushly uniformed occupant awoke.

"Henri, I swear that one day you will goad me and it will be too late..." He roared as he flung open the door, but as soon as he saw Vivvy, he was stunned into silence. "Oh, please pardon me, miss!" He swooned, and took her hand and kissed it as if he would eat it. "You must forgive an old army man who has been woken up so suddenly." I smiled. He was positively gushing. "Please come inside, both of you. Henri, charge the fares of these two young people to my account and bring us some coffee, wine and food. It is my pleasure." Henri smiled wearily back at the Major, and departed. At least for a while, I thought.

We entered the compartment at the Major's flamboyant hand gesturing and sat down. I wondered if my presence was an inhibition to him; as if he were disappointed because I was there, because when we were actually seated opposite him in his reserved compartment, after all the thanks and other introductory pleasantries had died down, the huge walrus of a man that was Major Benoît Allais, fell into silence. But then suddenly he erupted into words like a volcano and just as loudly,

"Okay, so what is happening in the outside world these days? Do people still have thoughts and opinions like they used to?" I had clearly misinterpreted his silence. I had thought he was inhibited by the presence of another male, even though he was by no means bashful in the presence of a beautiful woman, but the truth was much more mundane. He was quite simply bored. But my thoughts returned to Vivvy. As I sat next to her, I could almost feel her sadness through her skin. Her silence, too, was deafening, coming as it did from someone who was forever talking, someone who definitely had thoughts and opinions about everything, and today was for her not a day for sharing opinions. But the Major continued before either of us could frame a reply, even if we wanted to.

"I am again so sorry," he blurted. "You must think I'm an old fool, saying such things as if I never venture out into the so-called real world – even if that is the sort of thing that many people believe I am expected to say. But that is not the case, you see. Oh no! I am genuinely concerned!" His eyes were wide and his face soft as he said these things. As I listened to him, even if he was bored, I decided that I believed him. Simple as that.

"A noble sentiment, sir." I answered, hopefully in a tender and respectful tone. I didn't want to offend our benefactor, after all! "But doesn't everyone..." With that, the compartment door was knocked upon. It was Henri the conductor with refreshments. He was clearly having a tough day. He looked tired and worn out. I rushed to my feet to open the door. I hoped that for him this journey marked the end of his working day. Silently, he placed his tray with everything that was requested neatly on the tiny table shoddily fitted under the window. Such were the thoughts of those who designed trains at the time. I decided to tip him generously, on behalf of the Major, too. Both men were impressed, but it was of course the Major who spoke.

"I declare, young man, you have a sensitivity and a sense of propriety beyond your years! You either are, or will be a great leader of men. Indeed, I prophesy it!" Henri uncorked the wine bottle and gave it to Major Benoît, who sniffed it with great delight. "Oh, my dear Henri! You have excelled yourself, today! Not only do you bring us the finest wine, but you provide me with good, wise and intelligent company. Thank you so much, my good sir!"

Henri smiled weakly back at him, and nodded. He seemed to do that a lot. Nodding, that is. "I will always try my best for you, my Major. Even in my present duty as now a humble conductor. But if you will pardon me, there are many other passengers on this train and I, of course, have to attend to them, also. Goodbye for now, gentlemen, and miss." We all smiled back and thanked him as he left.

For the rest of the journey, we enjoyed the food, the coffee and the wine and pleasant conversation with our unusual provider, temporarily forgetting our respective situations. Vivvy smiled at him sweetly as he talked perhaps a little too loudly. This was for the Major, as you can imagine, a mighty encouragement. But as journeys must always do, this one came to an end. In our mutual departures, the Major was pleasant, modest with our gratitude, but not overly indulgent with us. We were both sincerely grateful to him, of course, but he did not linger, or, for instance, ask us to accompany him to wherever he was going, and so he left us.

Major Benoît Allais is yet another memorable character I wish I had known better. I also wish I had known more about the relationship he had with the humble conductor, Henri. I suspected that they had done military service together, at Henri's reference to him as "my Major". I'm sure also that there are many untold stories, between the two of them, and as individuals. And yet, wistfully, at the same time I absolutely knew even then that I would never meet either of them again. And for me, this strange atmosphere, which was both beautiful and sad at the same time, marked not only the end of a train journey, but the beginning of the end of my French adventure.

Neither Vivvy nor I had officially terminated our employment at Argent Port De Bluff. I have often wondered, even after all this time, if Robert, his son, his grandson, or some other descendant, or whoever, still waits for me to return! But as we stepped down on the platform at Ville de Reines, it seemed to me that with Vivvy a light had gone out somewhere deep inside her soul. We quickly found a small and reasonable hotel, and settled down. Yes, I knew it was by far no holiday, but as soon as we were in our room, Vivvy lay down facing the wall on the room's only bed, curled up into the foetal position, covered her face with her hands and sobbed. I really hadn't bargained for her being this bad. I laid myself down behind her, put my right hand on her shoulder and kissed the back of her neck. I had no idea of what to say. I knew of old not to ask her to talk, but this time, I really wanted to know for my own sake why this was all happening. True, Sonia was no angel, but I could not believe that she was that bad, even if she had been into some pretty mad things. Time had passed. Sonia was now a grown woman too. Perhaps it was my lack of experience surfacing, but nothing made sense to me. Her voice broke into my thoughts suddenly.

"You can have no idea what this woman is like!" She howled into her hands, without changing her position at all. "I wish I could explain, but I obviously cannot!" This only served to make me even more confused and desperate for an explanation, but now I had suddenly abandoned all hope of ever obtaining one. Without saying a word, I patted her shoulder, but she shrugged me away. I would, of course, never even attempt to say that everything was all right. It was entirely inappropriate. And not to mention, a lie. It felt to me like we were running for our lives. But why?

Calling the police was not an option for Vivvy, even though I had reminded her that if Sonia was under care as a mental health patient, her absence from that care amounted to escape, and for that reason, the police could be contacted. But that was, and remained, out of the question for her. Her only action was to send a telegram to her mother, explaining the present situation and to ask if we could stay with her for a week, maybe two.

Meanwhile, back at Argent Port De Bluff, things were also happening.

After the previous night's debauch with Sonia, Bernard realised that I was missing too, and had started looking for me, and in a sense consequently, looking for Vivvy too. And that, of course, had been Sonia's plan all along. She had become a regular thing in Bernard's life, and in particular, his bed, when at a time carefully chosen by Sonia, she would ask, and Bernard would oblige her with all the information he had gleaned. After all, as far as Bernard was concerned, everything was fine. There was nothing wrong with anyone, and he had found a sexy French girl to share his bed. For him, life could not be better. He ate his meals at the cafés on the village square, had met up with Mimi and Robert, who had given him some general information. But, both Robert and Mimi began to demonstrate a wise reluctance towards him. It had become evident that the now long-standing visitor was asking too many questions. Mimi could answer practically nothing. All Robert knew was that they had both left the village for a short while, but he had no idea where they would go. This was for Bernard totally annoying, but not for Sonia. She was aware that her cousin's options were few. She had gone to Vale to spread her wings, only to find that at Vale they were daily being clipped, never anticipating or even imagining that she would be trained and disciplined. The Little Lost Girl, as everyone else liked to call her, was caged at Vale. But she was, as far as Sonia was concerned, a spoilt brat. Everything that the family ever did, yes, everything, was for the Little Lost Girl! Now, all the little bitch could do was go back to Mama. But life had moved on and maybe, after a time in this ideal little place, she was either feeling even more lost than ever, or, as might well be so, especially now as she had now found yet another boy to keep her warm at night, there was a clear and definite possibility that she might go with him. This would have both advantages and disadvantages for her. Advantage, because her mind would be too clouded by the amorous to think clearly, and thereby keep her from taking any positive or decisive action. But for Sonia the only and great disadvantage was simply not knowing for sure where, out of her limited choices, she would be most likely to go. As far as this man Bernard knew, they had only left temporarily, but that was uncertain, because the family had poisoned Vivvy's mind against her. This was agony! She would need working on, if only temporarily, but how?

Then a breakthrough.

Of all the things that he could possibly have said, the man, Bernard, told her that the boyfriend was British! It was now for her suddenly so easy! Now, all she had to do was follow the foreigner! They stood out so starkly, even though this one spoke natural French! Tonight, she would work Bernard, this man who thought he had a girlfriend, into a frenzy and just before that *special moment* came, would stop, lie still and simply tell him what she wanted. And he, who was already putty in her hands, would be immediately obsessed with getting it done and getting it done right. She smiled with self-satisfaction at this. Soon, adopted sister or not, she would be on her side!

In Ville de Reines, there followed two days of meaningless walking about while impatiently waiting for Vivvy's Mama to send a reply telegram. She was really worrying me, now. It was no use trying to look like tourists, because we simply did not. This was certainly not, as far as I was concerned, a place that had any power to even attract tourists. Vivvy was becoming very depressed, and made the abstract observation that I did not look foreign enough. I had no idea what that meant, or why it should be important. Quite an achievement, though, considering I had been in France for a relatively short time, but was sufficiently successful in blending in so well. We made a very odd sight, indeed. We hardly made any conversation with anyone at the hotel, or even in the village, for that matter. It seemed, and in fact was, her only purpose in life to get that infernal telegram. Just remember, this was a time without mobile phones or internet, or texting. Eventually, I suggested that we make the journey to her parents' home and just hope that they would be there. It seemed a good idea to me at the time. After all, we lived with great thrift and I was afraid that we were running up a very large hotel bill. This was completely unnecessary, as far as I was concerned. And so what, if her parents were away. They were her parents, for goodness sake! Everyone in the neighbourhood would know her, and we would have somewhere to stay until they came home. But alas, even that was not to be. This situation seemed highly loaded. To start with, Sonia may have been bats-in-the-belfry crazy, but she was not stupid. Then, there was the subject of her parents. It made no sense to me at all that their one and only daughter would or could only be allowed access to their home on the sole condition that she was first invited! If they happened to be away, that's life!

A Surprise Intervention

Many are the paths we take through life, and we embark upon them largely through the choices we make. Obviously.

But not always.

Jean-Luc Pinchon looked dirty and tired when he checked in to our hotel, and when we saw him, we were instantly encouraged when we realised that this was not a hotel for tourists only, and that we probably would not have such a large bill after all. He brought in no bag or case. He simply gave his name to the man at the desk and slouched his long limbs down in a hard wooden armchair in front of the bar and ordered a glass of wine – he insisted on the house red for the day, even though it was now early evening. The man tending the bar and taking the reservations filled a large glass for him. After Jean-Luc had taken a long drag at it, and, when he arguably looked and most likely felt refreshed, he took a deep breath, sat up in his uncomfortable seat and looked around the room to see what he could see. We were the only ones to be seen. He smiled at us with his dirty, tired face.

"Okay, so do you mind if I join you, please?" We both smiled back and said certainly. Yes of course. Without another word, he heaved his tall, skinny frame up to his feet, and bringing his drink with him, sat more comfortably down on the vacant chair the other side of our table. He sighed and smiled a tired smile. He looked happier in a soft seat. We shook hands and kissed and exchanged names and pleasantries about our lives. He was surprised when I told him I was British, because my French was so good. I did not even sound like a foreigner trying to speak it, especially as I had never taken a single lesson. The man at the bar came around to us and filled our glasses, uncorked another bottle of wine for our table and waved at us tiredly and dismissively. He shrugged and said it was okay. He was just making sure that we were all right, because he wanted to settle down on his seat outside in the evening sunshine. He said he was amazed that we did not want to do the same. We shrugged at him and said we were okay. Jean-Luc also shrugged and said that he had been driving out in it since before dawn and was ready for some indoor peace. The barman wordlessly agreed with a single nod, left and took his seat outside.

Jean-Luc was a gentle, tall, thin, quiet, unhurried Frenchman. Aged thirty-seven and married to Anna, who gave birth to their two beautiful daughters, he made his modest living driving his beat-up, old Citroën truck around all the local farms, and from there to the nearby towns and villages, helping them to get at least some of their produce to market. Usually, it was animals and vegetables. But now was the hay season and the going was tough; this meant not only long runs, but repeatedly long runs. And there was all the lifting, too. He always tried to work out which of these was the hardest, and how much longer his little truck could take the punishment he was giving it. But for now, at this precise time, all he knew was that it was time to rest and have some wine before going to sleep for the night. Sleep would not be easy tonight without his Anna, but he would do his best. He knew that dear Anna would understand his absence for one night. It was the hay season, after all. He would be home tomorrow night and everything would be as it should. I smiled warmly at him. He seemed to be a man after my own heart. He had seen something that needed to be done and, discovering that no one else was doing it, promptly set about doing it himself. It had by no means made him rich, but it had most definitely made him happy. I wished both him and his Anna and their two daughters a long and happy life together. He smiled deeply and inwardly at this benediction, and in silent response, he leaned forward with his glass in hand and we chinked our glasses together again to seal it.

He asked us about ourselves, and did we look forward to the same thing as I had wished him. I shrugged and said that I didn't know. Maybe if he had asked me that question a week ago, the answer would have been very different. But now, who knows? Then Vivvy whispered something in my ear. Jean-Luc laughed.

"I think you are wrong!" he said with a broad grin on his face. "Sweet nothings already! Ha!" He raised his glass again. I looked furtively at Vivvy and then at Jean-Luc. In that moment of hesitation we all have when we struggle with what to say and how to say it, I decided to jump in feet first.

"Would you mind taking us to the next town in the morning, please?" It felt like someone else was saying it. My natural British reserve was coming into play, I thought. But without a moment's thought, Jean-Luc got up and went to the bar and fetched another bottle of the wine we were all enjoying.

He filled both our glasses, then his own, thus emptying the bottle, and stamped it down hard enough on his return to the bar to make the sleepy barman still seated outside hear it. Without a sound or rising from his seat or even turning in any direction at all, he simply raised his left arm as a minimum acknowledgement of his awareness of the situation of his customers. Fully understanding this, Jean-Luc returned to sit down at his chair. Then he raised his glass again.

"Anywhere you like. Consider me at your disposal," and we chinked glasses once more for the last time.

The following morning, I paid the not-too-expensive bill I was hoping for. In this strange atmosphere that contained for me a combination of dreamy, unhurried French concourse together with more than a hint of melancholy, we were served a hearty French breakfast in the company of a cleaner and wide awake Jean-Luc. Vivvy had been to the post office very early and had managed to collect from there the long-awaited welcome telegram from her mother. I don't know how she had possibly managed it. I was under the impression that the post office was not open until much later, also that they would have delivered it immediately upon its arrival. But she was obviously a very resourceful girl. Seeing the telegram seemed strange. It was as if it had deliberately waited to arrive only until we had stopped waiting for it. We ate our hearty breakfast together, the three of us, picked up our miniscule luggage and headed out onto the pavement outside.

Jean-Luc's truck was a sight to behold. Whatever could be said for the quaintness of it, or even that it was a classic French icon, the truth was that the poor thing was absolutely filthy and probably not even roadworthy. Perhaps this explained his promptness in offering his services so readily, that he never really expected us to take him up on his invitation. I really don't know. But Vivvy loved it and told me not to be so stupid when I tried to warn her about it.

So, clutching the much anticipated telegram, the contents of which had yet to be revealed to me, all three of us crammed ourselves into a driver's cab that looked like it was only designed for one and a half people! We set off, I knew not where, on a bright sunny morning in the early autumn that looked more like summer. As we drove along, I realised how much I had enjoyed all this. I mean all of it. The launching out, the different country. Everything. How much my life had changed and in so little a period of time. We were squeezed in the tiny cab, myself like piggy in the middle, with Jean-Luc to my left, and myself twisted in a side-ways position to my right, with my body facing Vivvy. She, facing right, hung her right elbow out of the window to try to make room. She actually seemed to be enjoying it! Oh, and did I mention that this quaint classic French icon had absolutely no suspension whatsoever? That's right! We felt every single stone in the road. By the time we arrived in a tiny hamlet called Chatoise, we were exhausted. Yet the whole trip had only taken about forty-five minutes. None of this seemed to have any effect on the good-natured Jean-Luc. We paid him what we considered fair and he agreed. Again, we shook hands and kissed, but I felt a strong pang when I said goodbye to him. As he drove away into the distance, I thought that there are many characters like him across the world, who are happy in their lot. I was left to wonder what the world would be like if more people were like Jean-Luc Pinchon.

The Telegram

Vivvy had changed. Since the arrival of the telegram, I had become increasingly of the impression that she was hiding something. I knew that her cousin Sonia was becoming for her, in her mind, a real problem and a growing threat, but what I could not work out was why this was so after so long a time. What did Sonia want? Why was Vivvy really so frightened of her that we both had to leave our jobs, maybe permanently, to get away from her? And could she really escape from her, if that was what she wanted? It appeared that we were going to her parents' home. But why? Why now were we going back to her parents? Why suddenly was it such a good idea after all this time? Where were her parents, if they were not home? Who had sent the telegram? If not her parents, was it someone else in her parents' stead? It was her parents who had sent her to Vale. Why did she have to wait for a telegram to come before she could go to her own home? Without actually seeing the telegram, none of this made any sense to me at all.

It appeared that there was an inheritance to be shared out between the two girls. This was told me after much asking and then, in a petulant, relenting *well-if-you-must-know* kind of way. As I well know, the hope of quick money makes people do things they would not even consider in so-called normal life. It's like being in a war. When my now famous turning point came, I met this mindset head on. Trust me, I know. This being the case, Sonia's escaping from a mental home was not, as far as I at least was concerned, such a strange way for her to behave after all, especially if she believed that she had an entitlement. Perhaps in Vivvy's mind, if she could get far enough away from Sonia, it would prove she was nothing like Sonia, but she was trying to get back to her parents' house as quickly as she could. *And so was Sonia!* Was this some sort of race? The little village we had arrived at was hardly the perfect place to get ahead of Sonia because it had no railway station. There were no taxis around, which is why we had to try so hard to get the lift here. And without our own car, I had no idea of how we would get any further unless we actually walked to wherever the next railway station was. Then Vivvy visited the post office again, and sent, she told me, yet another telegram to her mother. This time to confirm to her that she would be coming. I demanded to see the first telegram. I felt I had the right, but she told me that she would show me after we arrived at her parents' house and had settled down and I would understand everything. After all, we would be there for a couple of weeks, at the least. When she told me that, my sense of unease increased. Nothing about it seemed comforting. I felt I was on the outside of it all. The more I tried to think about it, the further away it all appeared.

I felt that all I could do was wait. Little did I really know.

We found a quiet café where we tried to relax and have something to eat. We sat at an outside table, where we could, hopefully, have a chance to talk things through, which talk I felt I badly needed. It was just at that moment, also, that I noticed that she was sitting opposite me. We always sat side-by-side to eat. It was one of our many unspoken things. We ate in silence at the nicely laid table.

"You're good at being French, aren't you?" she said, arching her back and replacing her cutlery. This was unpleasantly new. The girl I had fallen in love with had been curious and uncritical of everything. She simply loved everyone.

"Do you enjoy it?" she asked. Her voice was clipped and sharp. A tone I had never heard. "Is it a form of entertainment to you? What are you escaping from?" It felt like she twisted a knife with every word. My eyes were wide and searching, and I felt completely lost. It seemed like she was a whole different person. She sat rigidly straight. I felt unable to speak. I wanted this time to ask her about the second telegram and what was going to happen regarding it, but all that felt like a million miles away, now.

Then a car of a dark silver, almost a gun-metal shine, pulled up in front of the terrace of our seating area. It was not a very large car, but looked sturdy, almost military in appearance. I looked for a manufacturer's logo somewhere, but found none. I found myself suddenly deeply curious about it, because it had parked right by us. The action looked quite deliberate. But Vivvy made no effort to even move for a while, and no one got out of the car. I peered inside for no reason I could figure out. What I saw left me confused and somewhat upset. The driver was a man I did not know, and the front passenger seat was empty, but on the back seat were Bernard and Sonia! I stood up suddenly, ready to protect Vivvy, notwithstanding her recent strange behaviour. But Vivvy was unmoved.

She calmly smiled up at me, then turned her attention on the car's occupants. All three of them smiled the same unearthly smile at her and each other. When I saw this, it was as if a light came on, and sudden strength with it. It was the telegram. This whole thing had not been an escape from Sonia at all. It was no more than a move to get me out of her life for fear that she would not have to share her inheritance even further than it already was being shared! As I remained standing, I stared down at her in an emotional cocktail of anger and despair. Financial gain had been the last thing on my mind with her.

"Okay. Why?" I said. In English, this time. "What have I done?" She remained silent, got up and walked deliberately slowly to the open front passenger door of the car.

"Do you really need an answer?" she said, in the same sharp, clipped voice. "Are you really that stupid? I wondered if you were that stupid, but for a long time I tried to convince myself that you were not. But really. Look at yourself, now." Then, without so much as another word, she sat down on the vacant front seat and closed the door. The car drove away.

I experienced an unreal calm at that moment. I simply, without thinking about anything, sat down and finished the meal I can no longer remember. I was alone. My darling Vivvy was gone, and so it seemed with her was my life in France. Everything else and whatever else was left, felt blank and numb. Maybe I would cry later, but I distinctly remember the fact that I could not feel anything. With the meal finished, I got up and paid the bill for us both. There was not a single word in my head. I was not thinking anything. There was not even mind-noise. Just complete inner silence. It was as if I was sleepwalking. What was there to work out, you might ask? Answer, plenty. For example, what had just happened? Why was I not with them? What was I supposed to do? My mind was not in turmoil. I did not feel heartbroken, or anything of that nature. I knew I had to get on with something, but what that something was, I had no idea. A beautiful French girl that I had known for over a year had calmly walked away from me, taking with her all my hopes of a happy life in France. After wordlessly paying the bill and equally wordlessly picking up my bag, I walked away out into the deserted street. I decided to try to find a taxi, but it was no use. Then I remembered how, when I first stepped off the ferry, I had prepared myself for the possibility of long walks and the prospect of sleeping outdoors and being pleasantly surprised that it did not happen and how happy I had been in Argent. I walked as I thought about these things and about how I maybe should return there, but to what? At first they would be surprised not to see Vivvy, and soon after the questions about her died down, everyone would feel so sorry for me. Then I felt it; that terrible sting at the bottom of my throat, and I knew my face was wet with tears and could in no way hold them back. I am not my father. I am not strong. I felt as if I was bleeding from my very inside out. I walked until I reached a lamppost, rested my back against it and sank to my knees, and cried like a little lost child. It was, of course, not long before a well-meaning passer-by stopped, tenderly put her hand on my shoulder and asked me if I was all right. I put my hand on her hand to silently acknowledge that I was grateful for her concern but also that she had no need to worry. It seemed at that time that no matter how hard I tried to speak, words would not come. I simply nodded to her, and stood up, as much to convince the stranger that I was all right as to gather momentum for myself. Maybe it was grief at my loss, or perhaps confusion about that loss happening in such a strange way. But whatever it was, I remained silent. I patted the stranger's hand again. I instantly felt her hand under my shoulder in her feeble but well-meaning effort to help me to my feet. Not wanting to put her under any strain, I made an extra effort and was soon standing straight. I brushed my hair and my shoulders with both hands and turned to face my helper. I smiled a very tired smile back at her.

"Merci beaucoup, Madame." I managed to say.

"Je suis sûre que tout va bien, jeune homme."

I smiled back weakly, nodded my head and walked away. As I turned away, I stared for a very brief moment at this calm, dignified woman, who appeared to me right then as so composed, as if she had both experienced and solved every problem in life; all I could think was that I had a lot of thinking to do. Like what had happened, and what to do next. But the right ideas would not come. It seemed that not even my own mind was talking to me. I simply continued to walk in the same direction as I had previously been. Everything had become different, but too suddenly so for me to manage it. I guess I knew that I would cope, even that I was coping, but I just kept walking. It was a good thing that the weather was still warm, but at that time I did not care. It could have been pouring with rain, and I guess that would have suited my mood, but it was not, and even that did not matter.

Suddenly, everything was now so very different. She had made it so. No, *they* had made it so. Also, I think that they had made it this way as soon as they met me. I had come here and it felt like a dream. Now, the dream had been reduced to a nightmare of despair.

Chatoise was a very small village with a post office, a shop that opened only three days per week, a small bar and a church, whose doors were never closed. Its entrance was guarded by a huge tree. You could not be blamed, if you are so inclined, for thinking that the tree was somehow hallowed, because in order to enter the church, you had to make a real effort to get around the tree. Yet no one had cut it down, or even suggested it. In the post office, there were postcards on sale of prints showing an old etching of the village square, which appeared exactly as I saw it, with the single exception of a young sapling growing up outside the church. I don't know why, but the issue of this tree had become very much a preoccupation with me. Something suddenly of the utmost importance. I treated it as a puzzle, and desperately wanted to solve it as soon as possible. But I was feeling overwhelmingly tired. Drained from my recent experience and continued walking, my mind returned to the inescapable immediate concern of where I would spend the night. As any man would do in these circumstances, I entered the little bar. It was around the left corner near the post office. It was a very old-looking place, which, with its yellowed walls, crumbling mosaic flooring and silence, was clearly meant to serve the meagre requirements of the villagers. I sat down and it seemed right that I should order a large beer, leaving the pursuit of wine for another time. There were four other men sitting around one table in the far left corner of the room. They stopped their conversation and waited until I had taken the first drag at my glass. At which point they raised theirs and smiled brightly, saying, "Your good health, young man." And, although I felt exhausted, nervous and weak, I managed to smile back as brightly as I could, raise my glass to them and returned their benediction. I apologised to them that because the bar was so dark, I did not see them when I came in. They laughed and told me not worry about such trifling matters and to come join them. Well, it was certainly true that some friendly, pleasant company would be just the right thing for me in that situation. I picked up my glass of beer and sat down with them. Suddenly, the place did not seem half as strange as it had a moment ago.

They were very friendly, but they were not stupid. They could see that I had a lot on my mind, so they talked about themselves and life in general. There was a factory about twenty-five kilometres outside the village (I have no idea to this day what type of factory it was, who owned it or even what goods it produced, and neither did any of them seem disposed to explain this salient piece of information to me) in which each of their wives worked. Also, they themselves worked there too. They were, it appeared, responsible for the maintenance of the building itself, the assembly line, which was the factory's life-blood, and driving the truck to transport goods and materials to and from the factory. They ordered more drinks and kindly bought me another beer too, for which I thanked them. When we were all seated again, they smiled at me, knowingly this time, and asked me why was a young man like me travelling alone and looking so sad. It was quite clear to me right there and then that I knew that my life might just be a story worth telling, but the thought was only fledgling at the time. So, with the comforting feeling of some quantity of beer inside me, I began. As I talked to them and watched them listen, I knew that my time in France was over. I had nowhere to stay the night and was ready to walk whatever the distance it was back to Ville de Reines and its tiny railway station, and from there back to Argent Port de Bluff. And from there? I rubbed my unshaven chin aggressively as I thought about this. The moment I did this, they got up and ordered more beers. I considered it my turn to pay, but they took a mild form of offence at this, as they considered me their guest. I turned in my chair to face the open door, and as I did so, I saw outside that it was getting dark, with the dim yellow streetlamps making my eyelids feel all the heavier. I knew this pleasantness could not last much longer. When I returned to my original position in my chair, I saw that I faced a fresh glass of beer. I must say that it certainly felt good. My fretful, drained feeling had thankfully largely disappeared. It was soon obvious to me that the temporary departure for the bar had formed some sort of demarcation in our social and conversational exchange, as they now considered it their turn to speak to me and impart their collective and personal life experience. It made no difference to them that I was not French. I could have been anybody and they would have the same advice for a man in my situation. You see, they were very good at this. Did I trust them? Well, yes of course! It was clear to them in my speech and my manners with them that I was completely at ease. Had I not allowed them to buy me these two glasses of beer out of respect for the fact that they had invited me to be their guest for the evening?

They told me to forget her and go home.

Don't worry about a room for the night. The old garçon at the bar here would help me, as he could see that I had been accepted by them. Now I understood. If I had paid for their drinks, it would have meant that they were *my* guests, and that I was here for the purpose of achieving something selfish. But that was the way with these men. They were far more sophisticated than their rough appearance and simple rustic manners suggested. And the barman was true to their word! In fact, he was even better. He not only allowed me to stay in his mother's room, who was away for the week, but in the morning he served me a hearty breakfast, then drove me to Ville de Reines, depositing me at the little railway station and leaving me with a timetable for that day. I was so grateful for all this. He flatly refused to take any payment, considering it payment enough that the men who most frequently visited his bar would not only have a foreign friend, but had welcomed him so warmly. It was a good thing for them to do. They would talk much about it, and this would undoubtedly encourage other people to visit his bar. And with those remarks, we shook hands, kissed and said goodbye.

I lifted the latch on the iron gate that was the station's entrance, entered, and making sure it was closed behind me, walked up the narrow grass slope onto the single platform. As I sat there alone, I decided it would be a good idea to study the train timetable, which I did for a short while.

But my mind wandered.

I was five stations away from Argent. I wondered what Robert would say when he saw me return alone. I had been happy there, but when I met Vivvy, it was like heaven on earth.

Until yesterday, that is.

Being with Vivvy made me feel like the happiest man on earth. She had filled all my thoughts. Everything about her was in the forefront of my mind all the time, even when I was working. This also included the times when I was so busy. I was not consciously aware that I was thinking about her. It was as if every conversation with a customer, whether visitor or local, was influenced by our being together. Even if I read anything silently to myself, I found that it was her voice that was reading it to me from inside my head. Sometimes, when I was talking to other people, without thinking, I would use her verbal expressions and mannerisms. Through her delicate persona and manners, she had taught me to see the world through gentle eyes. And I felt like a better man for her friendship.

But then, on the little raised terrace outside that tiny café in Chatoise it all changed so suddenly. In a split second, I found that I could not make sense of anything anymore. We all like to know the end of a story, and I was aching to know the end of this one. But everything was suddenly taken from me, and nothing but questions flooded my mind. Vivvy had obviously had a prior knowledge of Bernard, but how? And the sight of her calmly getting into the same car as Sonia: this was something that I just could not understand. And who was the driver? And where were they going? So many questions.

And so many years. About thirty-five years have passed and I still don't know the answer to them. I have never, and this is what tears me apart, heard from Vivvy since. And this is something I desperately wanted to do.

The abrupt noise of the oncoming train brought me back to the present. I crumpled the as yet still unread timetable very quickly into my pocket, grabbed my small bag and hurried on board. This time, the train was almost empty. This meant that there were hardly any reservations, and so I had no problem finding a compartment and a seat. But then again, this time I had had the good fortune to have boarded at the economy section of the train. I instantly found a compartment with only two people inside. They were seated apart and were not talking. One was reading a newspaper and the other was smoking. I entered without knocking. They took no notice of me as I settled down; then I realised that I had to make up my mind quickly where I wanted to go before the conductor arrived. I flattened out the timetable on my lap and studied it. It appeared that I was on The Northern Route. It had started on its journey two stations ago, at a place called Étang Serein. There were five stations between Ville de Reines and Argent Port de Bluff. But then I spotted that last station beyond that and I felt like I stared at it for ages. I just could not help myself. Argent was not the last station. As I looked down at the crumpled timetable on my lap, I sighed, quite tearful. I knew that the two stations were not too far apart, because the day I first got off the ferry I had walked the distance.

That other station was Port de Ferry. It read like this: Port De Ferry – *Prend Fin*.

Those last two words held me in their grasp.

Prend Fin. Journey's end

I could feel something welling up inside me, and I knew, I just knew, I had to take The Northern Route to the journey's end. I slid my bag gently and slowly under my seat with the back of my right heel and settled back, but sleep was impossible. I felt so alone. I don't even remember the conductor coming and collecting my fare. I stared out of the window longingly and studied everything in detail, every blade of grass, every shaft of sunlight, every little solitary house, every village; then there was a cluster of two or three houses, a warehouse, a church – everything was so beautiful.

But the worst part was when the train stopped at Argent Port de Bluff. How badly I wanted, not just to stay there, but for everything to be just as it was the day we had left it! How simple and *precious* it would have been to step off the train and walk through the rickety old gate at the end of the platform and to find Vivvy waiting there and telling me not to be such a silly Englishman. Or for that matter, to have woken up in our tiny, lovely, so cosy room next to her and find that all this had been nothing more than a bad dream! But the train pulled away while I was thinking this, and after the two other passengers left, tears ran freely down my face, because I knew that I could not face life in Argent without her. It would never be the same, nor could be. It seemed that everything beautiful was being taken away from me.

Au Revoir France.

Return To Britain

It was such a body blow. Visibly, seeing the smallness of my old home after experiencing *the outside world*. But then, emotionally. Seeing the house so empty and silent was definitely not helping my state of mind. Yet I was glad that, in spite of being empty for so long, squatters had not moved in. If I'm honest, I have to admit that a few pangs of self-pity made my parents presence felt, but the immediate practical concerns that had to be attended to forced me to push these feelings to one side. I still had difficulty thinking of it as *my* house. As far as I was concerned, it had Hawkey written all over it and always would have. Nothing wrong with that. Yet it had still fallen into a state of disrepair. It was fit for habitation, as far as I was concerned, but many jobs needed to be done. Like some wiring and plumbing, but also a lot of decorating. These were, thanks to my newfound experience, within my capabilities, so I set about them with a positive state of mind and a definite sense of purpose.

My old neighbours were all glad to see me back. They told me that I had never looked better and wanted to know all about my adventures in another country. You would think I had been to Outer Space, and I must admit that, when I spoke to them about it, everything I told them compounded this idea. That it was not far had no relevance for them at all, but even for me it seemed like another world when I was back home. Yet another invitation to tell the story of my life, I thought curiously. All this was carried out in a communal, sociable and light-hearted frame of mind over a few pints at The Sun Inn. A relatively modern place in the village, it had been converted from the old billiard and snooker hall. It was there that I told them my stories, glossing over the hard parts, as we all do. I showed them my photos and postcards, and tried to sound as knowledgeable as I could about little things that I had gained some experience of along the way. And to be sure, they were duly impressed. Then I relaxed and allowed them to tell me some of the many things that had happened in the village during the time I had been away. I had for myself noticed several differences already. The Co-Op was certainly not the overarching presence it used to be. Also, the Social Club, so much loved by my parents on a Saturday night, was gone – not even the building remained. When I asked about that, they told me it burned down. It had gone downhill fast as soon as the pubs started. There was only this one here, but elsewhere they were all over the place, and young people being young people... Between us, they said, we think it was an insurance job. After they cleared the ground, they built a mini-market there. And everyone loves that. We felt really posh walking around there, you know. All these idle pieces of information and chit-chat helped me enormously in the settling-in process, and we were very relaxed with each other. As we spent time with each other, the atmosphere grew more and more pleasant.

So pleasant a place was it, in fact, that I managed to pull a part-time job there! Four nights a week! Well, I'd had plenty of experience. International experience, too. I must say that the pub itself was busier and louder and more claustrophobic than the bars I had been used to in France, but I didn't mind. I got on with my work and went home after I was finished. No problem.

This helped me more than I realised. Since leaving France, I missed Vivvy so much, and it was so intense. How would I cope? But my old neighbours saw to it that they always talked to me, if not on the street, over the garden fence the old-fashioned way. They would also invite me to lunch every now and then, which I thought was very kind of them and told them so. Together with this was the general condition of my house and the work involved in bringing it up to standard. There was no rush, as far as I was concerned. I had money saved from my work when I was away, I had neighbours that I had known all my life, I had a pleasant part-time job and I had plenty to do at home. Life was nothing but a dream, right?

Wrong!

Wrong, because no matter what I did, whether it was spending time with people or working at home, the fact remains that if you are alone, especially after a girl like Vivvy, the pain always comes back. It never goes away, *Never!*

I worked twice as hard at home. I was really proud of myself. I stayed at work a long while after my shift was finished. Everyone thought I was very generous. I was accommodating with tradesmen, and they told me I was very helpful. Maybe I ought to come work for them! But it was all a vain attempt to stay in company.

Eventually, we all went home from work, I signed for the deliveries, and the tradesmen drove away. There was no avoiding it. I was alone! This was precisely what I had been dreading while I was sat out on the deck of the ferry when I was leaving France. Eventually, my despair began to show. The conversations at The Sun Inn were different. Here, unlike Argent Port De Bluff in France, there was not a constant flow of visitors. The term "regulars" was the main idea here. And local gossip, the weather and the cost of living were the only subjects of conversation.

Then came the night when I decided to leave for home as soon as my shift was finished. They must have thought it strange, but I didn't care. It was also the first night that I noticed that I did not have a television. That also brought a pang to my throat. After my mother's death, I returned the old analogue colour TV to the Co-Op. It was something I had not even given a second thought to. Yet on this particular night, its absence was as plain as a pikestaff. I wouldn't have cared what was on, just to have the sound of other people's voices in our house again. I closed the front door behind me and without even removing my jacket, sat down in the armchair that was my father's favourite. It was so quiet; I couldn't stand it. As I sat there, I felt more seasick than I ever did on the ferry. I missed Vivvy so much!

Then, a thought struck me with a horrifying blow: tomorrow there was nothing to do at all. Something had to change and it was down to me to make that change. But what that change was, I just couldn't work out. I thought of going back to France. Of course I did. Maybe even rent this house out, and move about just like Bernard said he was doing. But I now knew that it was a lie. His whole persona was a facade that was concealing something that he, Sonia, Vivvy and the other man driving the car, the man I didn't recognise, were planning together. But even that was never going to change the way I was feeling. Then I realised that I was thinking too hard. A simple solution was all that was needed. Maybe something as simple as buying a television set. No, I decided, that was definitely not it. I would be staying home all day, without ever going out, only to let loneliness destroy me. I just couldn't think of what to do. I stood up, hung my jacket in *the passage*, switched the lights off and went upstairs to bed. I decided that what was needed was a good night's sleep to clear my head.

It worked like a charm. The following morning, that simple solution was right there waiting for me to wake up!

Get A Job

My father, as I have said, never applied for a job in his life. He saw life's changes as new opportunities, and took them as they crossed his path without a qualm. And yet, quite how such a life philosophy led to breeding dogs for pit fighting is yet another of my life's remaining unanswered questions. It was my lot in life, so it seemed at that time, to have to resort to something more mundane and far less imaginative. That meant something as simple as applying for a job and attending an interview.

I was quite proud of myself on the day of this particular interview. Perhaps you might think I should have been nervous. After all, it was actually, amazingly, my first formal job interview. My time in France had definitely not brought riches, but had definitely succeeded in bringing about an eccentrically bohemian lifestyle which I loved. My whole purpose being, not the acquisition of wealth so much, but to travel and enjoy life. And yet I still held strong private aspirations in that direction. So, having travelled and tasted at least some of the enjoyment of life, as well as sorrow, on my return home, and directly as a result of Bernard's influence, I decided to do what for me at least, at that particular time, came somewhat naturally.

I became a salesman.

I enjoyed meeting people and being busy to the point of chaos. But what to sell? It was 1983, and having lived in the heady café culture atmosphere of small-town France, my self-consciousness on coming home was that of something of a sophisticate, so I chose to sell something I considered new, modern and sophisticated.

I chose to sell computers. But please understand... that what passes for computers now, compared to what passed for *computer* in 1983, is like comparing a modern day internet tablet to a hammer and chisel!

I knew absolutely nothing about computers. They were becoming more popular because they were eventually being considered as a potentially useful tool in the use of a large business – nothing small, obviously! A small business would never have need of such a thing as a computer for goodness sake. Come on, get real! That they might eventually be the number one must-have item for virtually everyone was something not even remotely considered. Nevertheless, it was my given understanding up to that point, whether true or not doesn't even matter, that if you were going to be a salesman, it was best to sell something you knew absolutely nothing about. The infallible essence about said *modus operandi* being that if anyone asks you a question (how dare they!), you can't answer them! All you had to say was something like: Sorry! That's not my particular speciality. Fiendish!

But, in those days, if you'd become a salesman because you considered it a serious career-type move, sort of thing (as opposed to a non-serious, fun, and reasonably quick access to money – sort of thing...), you're dead in the water already. Mine, as I say, was none of the above.

I did it because it was, for me, what came naturally.

Now, if you're simply doing what comes naturally, like I was, you will be able, because you're an on-your-feet-thinker-type, to talk your way out of anything. And guess what? It worked! Well, it did for me, anyway. And I dare say, for many others like me, once again, at that time. In fact, it worked so well, I decided to go solo.

A note of caution, here. A word of advice. When things are going well, never, ever, go solo.

Everything carried on as normal. I continued to place advertisements. I continued to phone for appointments. I continued to know absolutely nothing about computers. Nor, to be honest, did I care, but customers continued to make their now obligatory response, as far as my living was concerned.

But the writing was on the wall. I had no one to tell me that I was doing well, or that I was rubbish, for that matter. I know it sounds odd, but when you're a salesman, and in the eighties especially, you needed someone to tell you that you're rubbish, even when you're doing well. It provides a necessary restraint on your self-confidence. Don't ask me why; you just do. Things continued to go well. I had no one to tell me I was rubbish. Such is life.

Have you ever woken up in the morning, and had the distinct feeling that everything was different, even though everything looks the same?

You have? Good for you! Because I did not.

The phone rang; same as usual. Everything fine. Some guy named Chris. Sounded normal; again, everything fine. Had a big order, and he really meant a big order, for components. Cash on the nail. Sounded even better;

everything extra fine. Everyone does components, don't they? Well, yes, of course! Chris was paying. Never argue with a man who wants to part with money, was a motto I'd picked up somewhere. Seemed to pretty much sum up the situation, right then. Things were just getting better and better! I felt like nothing could go wrong.

But the world had changed Even though it looked the same.

Here's what happened. I have typed this from pure memory. It's not the sort of thing you forget, as you will see.

We met in Asda's car park. "To sort things out." I got into his car. The conversation went something like this:

Chris: (It would be an understatement to say that it's obvious that Chris works out. He was pure muscle. He looks big enough and hard enough to be the devil's bouncer) Have you got the components? I thought we agreed.

Me: (Nervously. I feel thin, pale and pathetic) Well, I only take orders.

Chris: (Takes a deep breath – obviously totally frustrated) I've travelled a long way for this. I represent some very powerful people. What is your price? Just name it. I'll pay you now. Cash.

Me: But I only take orders.

Chris: (snorts and laughs humourlessly) Don't we all... Get out! (He leaves the car. I follow him to the boot, which he opens. Inside is a single, huge, twelve-inch-deep briefcase. He pushes his jaw forward, clearly showing that he has lost his patience.) You had better be glad I am of a calm disposition! (He spits the word 'disposition' and punches the side of the car.

Screams:) What! Is! Your! Price!

Me: (Pleading with him, now) I don't know! Until you tell me what you want, how can I possibly give you a price?

Chris: (His eyes are bulging wide with anger.) What! Don't tell me you don't have them! (Grabs the briefcase and opens it. To my horror, takes out a huge pistol that looks to me as if it's made of aluminium and stuffs it into his belt, cowboy-style. I am terrified. He holds the briefcase open to me. I am shaking uncontrollably, in a state of total shock.) £360,000. Cash! Tell me, does the sight of a lot of money upset you?

Me: Yes, quite frankly (I don't know where the courage comes from. It is as if I am hearing someone else speaking, not myself) – I simply place the advert, receive the system requirement and call back with a price. If this is acceptable, I receive a deposit and arrange delivery. Once the installation of the system is complete, I receive final payment. That is what I do!

Chris: (spits at me) Another gopher! (As he says this, the unthinkable happens. He had been holding the briefcase in his left hand. With his right hand, he grabs the gun but thankfully does not remove it. Bellows at me:) Get back in the car! (I obey and return to the passenger seat of his car. He slams the boot closed and throws himself heavily into the driver's seat.) Right. Listen, and listen good. Here's how it works, no matter who says what. Research and development. You research. I develop. Simple. Things, the so-called components, are, once in a while, in spite of state-of-the-art security systems, lost. Manufacturers insure themselves against such loss. This is where you and I come in. You are the research, and I am the

development. I'm here to buy back the missing components.
Cash. No questions asked. I am here with the cash. You are
here without the components. My conclusion is, you lied.

Me: (My mind is numb. Gibbering.) I've not lied! (Still
terrified, I notice he has not removed his hand from the gun.)
You still haven't given me a chance to say anything! All I do...

Chris: (In a second, the gun is in my face – about three
inches away, making me see double. Madly, I think that if he
fires, he will burn his hand. Convinced I am about to die, I
commend my soul to God. He roars at me) Get out!

Me: (I obey)

Chris: (He drives away slowly)

That was the last I ever saw of "some guy named Chris".

I have never wanted anything to do with computers after
that.

Well, you simply cannot stand still after an experience like
that. I prided myself on being very resourceful when the
circumstances demand. And after the "some guy named Chris"
episode, demand is what the circumstances certainly did, with
great big bells on!

I decided to answer an advert this time, and see where it
would take me. If you don't mind, please allow me to give you
some advice. If you are going to be a salesman, go to a "Cash
And Carry", buy some stock and sell it. Much simpler as you
have both seen and are about to see. In fact, come to think of
it, I really did launch forth and answer quite a few adverts. The
experiences that ensued would amaze you. In fact, they
amazed me; both at the time and thinking about them after the
event. Although by no means exhaustive, here are a few for

your delectation:

Transfer Housing.

There was no actual interview this time. It was work "from home". All you had to do was find people who wanted to rent homes. Nothing difficult there, surely. Once you had found them in sufficient numbers, you place them in the hands of your boss, who would then allocate them appropriately. Once in residence, the tenant would then pay their rent. Then, as they continued in residence, they would potentially be allocated points for various things. Things like prompt payment, the healthy state of their rent account, and so on. Certain other points would be equally potentially awarded for the voluntary upkeep of the property, thus motivating the tenant towards a mindset of responsibility, rather than one of simply getting the longsuffering landlord to carry out all the work at his expense. But the best part was the last part: after twenty-five years, the title deeds were *transferred* back to the tenant. It all sounded wonderful. But I declined, wisely so, too, it seems.

As not one financial transaction had any recourse whatsoever to The Bank Of England, before my boss could allocate one tenant, would have paid me a penny in commission, or, for that matter, be arrested and charged with money laundering, he was found lying face-down on the beach outside his Isle of Man mansion. He had been shot twice in the back of the head.

Diplomatic Immunity.

The initial meeting was at a high-end London hotel. By an organisation clearly setting out to impress. No smiles. All serious. Stress dressing. The communal collection of facial expressions combined to send out a single message, and that message was: "We don't mess about." In actual fact, to be fair to them, it sounded like a golden opportunity. I would be, as part of a team, (you are Team Player, right?) selling custom-made limousines to the Sub-Continental Diplomatic Services. These would be bullet-proof, bomb-proof, and with, believe it or not, a wooden chassis (this was a safeguard against rust – amazing). Did I know anything about custom-made limousines, I was asked. No, I replied, in my confident manner, but I knew a ready-made market when I saw one. I was instantly accepted. The commission was £500 per order. I took to it like a duck to water. It was half the job to keep count of how many I was signing up.

Sadly, in spite of being told I had earned record commission, a luxury car for myself, a Mediterranean cruise with all expenses and spending money, I received nothing. Again, such is life.

The Man Who Would Be Al Pacino.

We were two people who were meant for each other. It was a rainy Tuesday afternoon, and the, er, *interview,* took place at a Greasy-Spoon café just outside Cardiff.

We had been through the same experiences of, oh you know, not being paid for work we had done, and that humdrum business of being threatened with the definite possibility of death for work we considered doing. In the then warped world of upside down thinking, there was, trust me on this here, something comforting about it. And our mutually compatible personalities put together the perfect business double act. The exit areas of local DIY stores would be our field of operations. *We* provided a service for people who, after visiting a DIY store and liked what they saw, decided to let someone else do it. And trust me, it is a fact of indisputable truth that Greg Morton certainly was someone else!

It was like taking candy from a baby. All I would have to do is wear a suit, and tap the departing customer on the shoulder (to me and Greg, the "prospect"), and, in a bright but polite way, say "Excuse me, please." They would then turn around to see a man in a suit and it was like they were freeze-framed. I would then give a very short explanation of our service. In the short time it took me to finish, they would be so relieved that I was not the Store Detective, that they would sign up for anything. Job done.

Me and Greg cleaned up.

Everything went like a dream. I was paid on time. No quibbles. Greg even gave me a lift to work when it was further away. I kept the work coming in; Greg got the work done. Money kept changing hands. Simple. Sweet. What could possibly go wrong?

Read on.

Greg, you might say, liked the sauce. In the same way that I had once tried *to* drink and failed, Greg tried hard *not* to drink and failed. Not that Greg was offensive or violent in drink; it was the case that when he was in this condition that he tended to bare his soul and reveal all. He was forty-two, divorced twice with no children, and now lived with his mother. His only escape was work. That was why we worked so well together; our mutual experience had made us workaholics.

Part of Greg's family was Italian, and when he would get onto some past grievance in conversation, he would break into an impersonation of Al Pacino in "Scarface" (his favourite film). This would go on for a while, until either a drinking partner, or his mother, or myself, would imitate him back and he would laugh at both us and himself, and everything would be well with the world again. Greg Morton's downfall, of which I am the sad witness, happened in three stages.

Stage One: As Greg's fortunes increased, his ex-wives filed for increased maintenance. Greg was convinced they would lose because there were no children involved. They won. The business was on the rocks, and my job with it.

Stage Two: One sunny winter's morning, we were driving through the South Wales Valleys in the Bedford Astra van that was Greg's only worldly possession, when Greg took his eyes off the road and stared wide-eyed and blankly into my face. His face turned grey, and he collapsed onto the steering wheel, shaking violently. I grabbed the steering wheel and tried desperately to pull on the handbrake, but there was not enough time; we crashed head-on into a stone wall. Greg had suffered an epileptic fit, and to make matters worse, also suffered a heart attack in the ambulance on the way to hospital. He was in a very bad way indeed. The van was an insurance write-off. I sustained whiplash and the loss of a great job.

Stage Three: Greg's mother died. Greg was no longer in business by then. He was unemployed and *on the sick*, as the saying goes, and although we stayed in contact, it was of course impossible to be the major part of his life that I once was. It was a very sad time. With no work to escape into, no one to laugh him back to reality and nowhere to call home (the house had passed, according to his mother's wishes, to an elder sister), Greg's life went into freefall. The police rang me one night, asking me to identify and vouch for him. This I did gladly. As I write, he is still under detention in police custody under the Mental Health Act. He has been in that condition for too long a time to be healthy for him, in my humble opinion, and yet, in spite of as much evidence as that, I refuse to believe that this is the end of Greg Morton. My heart goes out to him.

Now, on with my story.

The Job of a Lifetime?

This time I decided to learn my lessons. And my decision paid off. It was literally like my own licence to print money. What was it, you may reasonably ask. It was very simple. No commission, no supervision, and every day was payday! There was even a dress-down policy into the bargain. It was selling health and wholeness magazines directly to the public. It was so good. I would have done it until I retired from it.

That is, if I had had my way.

Oh, the golden valley of Rhondda! I had decided to go out selling in all weathers. You might even say that I drove myself very hard, but that was not the way I saw it. Obviously, it was the best way to make money at what I found myself doing, but, you see, when the weather was good, that is, bright and sunny, people answered their door in a happy-to-see-you frame of mind. They then paid the princely sum of one English pound very gladly and I left them and went on to my next potential customer. And so on and so forth. But when it was raining, it was even more in my favour, because when someone answered their door on a rainy day, they seemed to instantly sympathise with me, being out in such weather, and for something only costing a pound after all. Aah, there there, deary. Here you are! On this particular fateful day, it had been raining all through the previous night, and I was in the process of giving my usual, and winning recital to the good lady of the house, when my foot slipped and I fell down her front steps. My last conscious thought, undoubtedly because I was in such enormous pain, was that I had broken both my knees. Fortunately, I had broken nothing. I had, however, badly bruised both knees and twisted my spine. I was kept in hospital for two nights as a precaution, and released on the condition that I took complete rest. The potential for the enjoyment of a well-earned rest was definitely dampened, knowing that I had lost my favourite job. I decided that things could not possibly get worse.

A note of caution, here. A word of advice. Never. Ever. With God as your witness, decide that things cannot possibly get any worse. Because, and you can completely trust me on this, that becomes the precise moment when they do. My fortunes stopped declining, and went into the next level of free-fall.

Which brings us very neatly to the day of the job interview to end them all.

The Partnership.

Yes, blissfully oblivious of what lay immediately ahead of me, I really felt proud of myself that April morning, because after having made a sound recovery from quite a serious accident, I was attending a job interview within a month. It was my favourite weather: bright and sunny and freezing cold. Selling weather. I felt confident. I was asked if I wanted a salary or commission. I chose commission. I was accepted. We obviously spoke the same language.

"Are you ready to make some serious money, Mark?" the guy with a nasal American accent said.

"Well, that's why we're all here, isn't it?" I smiled. We shook hands aggressively in the way that it seems to me that Americans insist on.

Yes. I was, I was, I was... ready!

The Partnership was an American company, specialising in providing financial services to people with low credit scores. This job lasted precisely twenty-two working days.

It was a season of pure hell on earth.

On the first day, my six colleagues and I were locked out. That's right. Completely forbidden entry. We were treated ignorantly, as if we were total strangers. What was all that about? Eventually, a man came to the door and tried to tell us we did not have a job. When we insisted, he told us to come back at 2.00 p.m. when he "would try to sort something out". We refused point blank. So did he, and slammed the door in our faces. We all went home, never expecting to return. Each of us received a telephone call later that same day, supposedly from America, apologising for the mix-up and promising higher commission. And, like the fools that we were, we agreed to return.

Sure enough, the following day, we all presented ourselves at the same door of the same building and in exactly the same manner as the day before. Though on this particular second day, we were greeted by the uniformed security guard, who did at least not turn us away ignorantly as other man had done. He said that he agreed with us that we were telling the truth, but had not been given any clearance measures because the tenancy contract documentation was not finalised. He promised he would make some calls, and sat us down in his quarters and provided us with refreshments while he sat by his desk and did as he promised. But it took more calls than he had anticipated, and, it seemed, the more calls he made, the longer they took. As time went on, our collective sense of frustration and despair was mounting, but at least this was better than yesterday. Eventually, he replaced the receiver with a huge sigh of relief and turned from his desk on his swivel chair to inform us that some temporary arrangement had been made, but not at this address. He hesitated as if waiting for us to guess where it was. We refused to try and simply asked him to hand over the piece of paper he was holding. We had watched him writing something down as he was talking, and when he finally handed it over, he did so as if surrendering it. It was very difficult to gauge his strange behaviour at that point, but when we saw what was written, we were amazed. Suite 423, The Pacific Monsoon Resort Hotel, West Lane. He looked at us amazed. We looked amazed in reply. Silently, we left.

The Pacific Monsoon Resort Hotel was not easy to find, but once we were in, we were escorted to the private suite by a short, strange-looking man with a simpering, apologetic manner, who then gave us all drinks and treat food, and encouraged us to stay motivated. Everything was arranged very carefully. We were each given a seat by a table with a single telephone, and told to make calls, using the script we were then promptly provided with. We were then taken through a rehearsal and brainstorming session, and then we actually settled into some kind of routine. How many deals could we make, that was the question. My personal average was nine deals per day. This was, to be fair, roughly the same as the rest of the group. Not much by way of persuasion was involved, because each of the prospects on our list needed the service quite urgently. If a man is unemployed and/or in debt, he knows perfectly well that he wants a loan, or a bank account with guaranteed overdraft, or a mortgage, or indeed, a low interest gold credit card.

But the whole thing was corrupt and unjust. No business was placed. Not one bank account was opened; not one loan arranged; not one mortgage processed; no one received a credit card. When we asked about this, we had the tort reply that no one had qualified, and were loudly and verbally chastened for our lack of sales talent in a market and with a product that, when everyone else tried it, they all said that it practically sold itself. What was wrong with us? We ourselves asked some serious questions about this, but quickly found this to be a very unwise course of action. We encountered outright hostility, to the effect of who did we think we were to ask questions in the first place? We had to remember, we were told, that apparently there were thousands of people out there just waiting to do our jobs, so just watch out, will you? We learned later that most of the callers did indeed qualify, but only the minority did not. So where was all the money going? This time, we got serious, but instead of asking questions, we made discreet, urgent enquiries, getting our information from the actual banks, building societies and loan houses. Said information provided by official sources set all the alarm bells ringing. We had been given the false impression that our jobs were simple and hassle-free. Also, that they were unregulated. To this, the emphatic reply was that there was no such thing. Searches are compulsory, and are to be carried out routinely. Then, and only then, is a client (note, client, not prospect) cleared for the service he requires. But that involves rigorous client questioning, form-filling, the surrender of highly personal information, and all this to be conducted by individually qualified consultants with banking qualifications and experience, thus ensuring that all business was carried out in accordance with the legal guidelines of the central financial policing organisation of the time. But this was the exact opposite of what we ourselves and all our prospective clients were led to believe. It was on hearing all this that we decided to team together, because it was obvious that all advertisements for contractors containing catch-phrases like "no experience needed", "like taking candy from a baby", "non-status" and "definitely no credit checks" were at least wrong and, much worse, probably illegal. Here is what we, as a group decided:

All the advertising that had been given, we assumed to be a lie. Credit checks had to be carried out by law and each potential client was told exactly that, but we will do everything to help you. We told them we were transferring them to Central Loans. At least that way, all the rest of their business would be carried out legally.

The working day on which these decisions were made was the twenty-second, and our last. We turned up the following morning to find the hotel suite completely vacated. The Partnership had disappeared off the face of the earth. We had not been paid. We called the police and individually appointed solicitors to act on our behalf.

This time there was without question a case to answer. As soon as we had discovered the extent of the illegality, indeed the criminality, of the situation, we handed over detailed notes of each and every phone call, and the actions taken. These, together with all previous paperwork, we submitted to the authorities. There was also far more serious evidence against these men than even we had imagined. In fact, so large was the case, that it was already being handled jointly by Interpol and the FBI. Under these circumstances, wherever they ran, there was simply nowhere in the world to hide. Eventually, they were all arrested. One in Alma, Sweden, one in Dresden, Germany, one on the Isle of Skye, Scotland, and the other in Las Vegas, USA. When they came to trial, they faced between them, just under ten thousand separate charges of fraud. They will never see the light of day again. In sentencing them, the judge told them that it was an enormous disgrace that men of such high intelligence, who had the natural gifts to excel at anything they chose to set their hands to, had chosen instead a life of crime.

This experience, and the others like it as related above, combined together to shout out one simple message:

There is more to life than this.

What was I to do? I felt clueless, desperate, lonely and depressed. It clearly felt like I had hit rock bottom. And after this? Well, there was only one possible conclusion, and that was that the only direction left to go was up. Things could not even possibly get any worse. Agreed?

Wrong. Wrong. Wrong.

The Claim Pack

My life was far from the best it could be. My depression had turned into anger, and my anger into rage, until it boiled over. Yes, it literally boiled over. Eventually, after this repeatedly happened, I decided that being as angry as this felt good. In fact it felt so good I gave it the name Esprit Fort (strong minded) and personified it, if you like. It felt like a friend, almost. I questioned everything. I couldn't keep the job at The Sun Inn, because of everybody there. All they did was tell me how sorry they felt for me and, never mind, buck up, and you'll be all right in the end. Tell me, just *what* on earth does that mean? But I never went off on one to them. I just quietly went home one night and didn't go back. No offence to them at all. Looking back, they didn't mean any harm. They just couldn't find anything constructive to say, and I simply didn't have the patience left to listen to any of them.

My biggest regret was leaving France. I felt at home there. I should have stayed there and toughed it out, even without Vivvy, and I'm sure things would have improved eventually. But that was another thing. I just couldn't stop thinking about her. I missed her so much. It was unbearable. I decided to go back to France. That was it. Final. Except for one small, but important thing: zero money. This was something that took me completely by surprise, that each of the business opportunities I had attempted was costing me money. Eventually, the drip-

drip effect of this finally made its presence felt. I had made the sad and undeniable discovery that I was penniless. I seriously thought of taking out a loan. I would borrow the minimum amount required, buy the fare on the ferry and return to where I was happy and a job that I firmly believed was still waiting for me. It sounded like a perfect plan. Yes! A loan it was! I even went so far as to apply for one. I told Mrs Cook at the building society, who was from the village and had known both my parents very well, that I didn't think I would be successful because I was unemployed. At this statement of disarming honesty, she smiled serenely and told me not to worry because the loan would be secured on my house. The actual name for it was remortgage. I sat back in the guest chair in her office and thought about this. After a couple of other questions I put to her, I understood that what I was doing was selling the house to the building society to get the loan, and that was the reason that they were so willing to smile pleasantly and tell me not to worry. They knew that the moment I was late with a payment, they would repossess my home. My *parents'* home! My father had paid cash for that house precisely because he knew he would never qualify for a mortgage, nor did he want one in the first place. The result was that he never had to pay a penny of the crippling interest charges, and I would never have to worry about having a roof over my head. I could feel Esprit Fort almost standing next to me, and I knew that if I didn't leave quickly I would lose my temper. I smiled weakly, stood up and left without another word. Mrs. Cook was very concerned and asked behind me as I was leaving if I was feeling all right. But I ignored her and left the premises. I don't think it was personal, that they were out to get me or anything, but at that moment, in the desperate frame of mind that I was in at the time, it felt like they *were* out to get me. My jaw was clenched and my face felt pinched as I walked down the street towards home.

"It's only across the English Channel!" I shouted after I was a distance away.

I was glad to get home, because I had worked myself up so much that I was seriously hungry by now. I had also walked about eight miles to save on bus fare. Bus fare!

As I opened the front door, I saw that there were a number of letters on the doormat and none of them looked friendly. Some envelopes were white, others were brown, but they all had windows. Wearily, I picked them up and carried them out to the kitchen, slammed them down on the table and wandered onwards to the tiny bathroom my father had built with his own hands. I closed the door and hung my jacket on one of the hooks inside it, just as both my parents and myself had always done. I washed my face and hands and thought of my parents, and things like, what would Vivvy have thought of this place? But then straight away I knew she would never see my home, that she would never come here and that I would never see her again! Despair rose up inside me until I felt full of it. How would I pay those bills out there on the kitchen table? What was I going to have for supper? So many questions without a single answer between them. I took a deep breath and went back into the kitchen. I stared at the letters on the old table. When I sat down, after a sigh that seemed to come from somewhere else, I began opening them one by one. I was right.

Bill after bill. I felt as if I had backed up into a small room inside my head as I read each one. Then I opened another letter. It was a brown A4 envelope. It was from The Employment Department. In it, I was informed that, due to my current employment status and its protracted period, I was required to attend an interview and state my intention to seek employment and have my eligibility assessed with a view, depending on the results, to claim benefits. It went on to advise me to think carefully about what I wanted to do, and that if I so choose to make a claim, to please sign the enclosed green application sheet, and either return it in the envelope provided or bring it to my nearest Job Centre, where I would receive a Claim Pack. My reaction to reading this was one of amazement and delight. So much so, in fact, that there was no way I was going to put it into the post. I had no idea how much money I would be able to claim, but it seemed like the perfect solution. I would simply claim this money, save up the fare to go on the ferry, then cancel it on the eve of my return to France. Heck! I would even rent the house while I was away! Talk about every cloud having a silver lining!

That night, I had the best night's sleep I'd had for ages.

Dawn rose the following day just as it has done every day of the world's existence up until now. To all intents, purposes and appearances, everything was normal. In fact, as far as I was concerned, better than normal, because I felt that I had gained another chance to make a life for myself. I washed and dressed, had my morning coffee, then foraged among the paperwork on my kitchen table until I found the letter from the Job Centre. While standing with my jacket on and ready to go through the front door, I decided to read it through quickly again, just to remind myself of its contents and make double sure that I had understood it correctly and make a mental note of any time that the letter specified. But I could plainly see that there was none. And in my mind at least, it meant that I was in no way obliged to visit them in any way, or to claim benefits at all. All I was going to do was to visit them and tell them what I planned if I was successful. I carefully folded the letter and equally carefully replaced it in its brown envelope, with my address on white paper showing through the window. I then folded it in half and put it in the left inside breast pocket of my jacket, straightened myself up in front of the long, narrow mirror in the bathroom and went out. Although I was penniless, I felt very optimistic.

The Job Centre was about six and a half miles away from my house, but I managed the walk in just under an hour. This was an entirely new experience for me. I had never been to a Job Centre before in my life, neither had both my parents, and as I came to think of it as I turned the corner onto the square, I knew of no one else who had. If this *was* the case, they had clearly kept it to themselves.

The Job Centre itself was not an unpleasant building, plain and functional, decorated in a combination of dirty blue and grey. It was quiet and unhurried, but, I felt, functional and businesslike. There were display boards with cards on them, which I was later to be told were the adverts of the jobs I would be applying for, and a single, long desk that occupied the whole length of the far wall opposite the entrance. Above it, suspended from the ceiling, were four cards, labelled 1, 2, 3 and Reception. I immediately made for the reception area. A serious but unthreatening woman, whose security badge informed me that her name was Angela, greeted me.

"Good morning, sir. How may I help you, please?"

"I don't really know, to be honest, but if I give you this letter, then perhaps you will be able to tell me. Thank you very much, by the way, for whoever sent it." I reached inside my jacket, took out the precious brown envelope and handed it to her. Without a word, she opened and read it silently for a moment. Then, placing my letter face-up on the counter to her right, she took a step back and searched with her eyes the contents of the shelves underneath, directly in front of her. Her eyes widened slightly. Clearly, she had found what she was looking for. She reached out with both her hands and dragged out a large transparent plastic bag containing several large documents. This done, she sidled to her left and took out a single piece of paper. She stood straight, and handed these items to me.

"Please write your full name, address, National Insurance Number and normal signature on the form provided. This is to acknowledge receipt of your Claim Pack. You have two weeks to complete and return it to this office, together with any other documentation and paperwork which may be relevant and helpful to your claim."

I put the Claim Pack down, took the pen she offered me, hastily completed the form and handed it and her pen back to her. A small whisper of anxiety seemed to brush past me like an invisible draught.

"Can I complete it now, please?" I asked. She smiled

thinly back at me.

"Mister Bashford, the Claim Pack takes a great deal of information gathering, as well as the providing of your personal information. And this is why you are allowed up to two weeks in order to complete it. You should also be informed that a shoddily completed pack will be returned to you and you will be asked to correct it, and you will appreciate that this will delay our processing of your claim. I strongly urge you to take the pack home, read through the guidelines and instructions, then complete it and return it to this office."

"Very well, then. I'll do my best." I felt the same anxiety return. I had wanted to tell somebody my plans, but I felt I was not going to get the chance yet. Meekly, I picked up the Claim Pack, placed it under my left arm, thanked her quietly and left the office.

Outside, it was a warm day and I found myself thirsty. I took a deep breath, because I knew that I could not afford to buy a drink from a vendor. A large bottle of supermarket brand soft drink was cheaper than a small can of theirs. I sighed. I would have to wait until I got home. I started to walk. As I did, all the anxiety questions surfaced. How could I do all this? How long would it take me? How long would it take them? How much money would I get? And of course, when could I go back to France? I felt so frustrated that I could not tell the lady behind the counter about this, because it was so special to me. As I continued to walk, the Claim Pack's plastic packing under my arm was making a wet sweat mark on the side of my jacket. I decided that I was fed up of it before I even got home, let alone before I opened it and tried to complete it.

When I did eventually get back home and unlock the front door and go inside, all I could think of was flopping the Claim Pack on the kitchen table. I stopped and stared at it for a while, even though there were other things I had to do directly as a result of coming in through my own front door. It was during this investigation, conducted in a breathless almost altered state, that I realised just how big the Claim Pack was. There were actual books in it. I wondered what information, personal or otherwise, these people would want. I sat down at the table. I was only vaguely aware that the front door was still open. I didn't care. Then I decided that the time for hesitation was over. I picked it up again in one hand to look for the opening, and was immediately struck by its weight. This was something I had ignored whilst carrying it home. No wonder I was tired, carrying it all this way! Not finding a visible opening, I tore at the plastic packing. It came apart surprisingly easily and soon I had placed all the paperwork neatly in front of me, separating the forms from the notes that I should be consulting as I proceeded. It is true to say that the sheer amount of paperwork, the complications involved in the process, the length of time that had been allowed for the completion, the businesslike manner in which I had been served, together with my simple but as yet unexplained plans, had stirred themselves into a cocktail of frustration in my head. Eventually I was able to understand the paperwork. I worked my way through it until I came to the part where two third parties would need to become involved. These were my bank, which in my case was the local building society, and my doctor. This was something that was lost on me. Why on earth would these people want to refer to my doctor? I decided to leave these blank until I had visited them and continued to wade through the forms, writing in the requested block capitals with a black ball-point pen. Slowly, page after page went by, until I had almost forgotten where I was. I was brought to a halt when I came to a page containing a large body of text, of which only half registered with me due to my tiredness and the aforementioned cocktail of frustration. I could see that there were still about two or three pages left, so I knew that I was not at the end yet, but relieved to know that I was at least getting there. It was when I read through the same page a second time, I was delighted that I was being asked to sign and date all the information that I had provided and was being warned of the consequences of providing false information. I scanned over the remaining pages to find to my equal delight that they were marked "For Official Use Only". I quickly signed and dated the form and placed it in the large brown envelope provided, of course without sealing it.

But the same whisper of anxiety brushed past me again. I shivered involuntarily and looked around. It was then that I realised that the front door was still open, and that I had done all this work straight upon coming in, without closing the front door, without taking my jacket off and without even having that much desired drink of cheap pop I had promised myself. I looked around the kitchen and found the bottle of lemonade and poured myself a glass. As I drank it, I realised I was shaking. Why, I asked myself. I snapped myself back into the moment, as it were, and looked at the clock on the mantle-piece. Ten past one. Not too late! I decided to visit the building society and the doctor straight away, then triumphantly return the completed Claim Pack to the Job Centre. Job done! I finished my drink, put the glass in the sink, picked up my brown envelope, walked back out, and this time taking care to lock the front door with the old familiar mortice key. With a determined air, I set off for the building society.

It took about forty-five minutes to arrive, but by that time, the building society was full. I could not have timed it more perfectly if I had tried. You see, by this time, the people in the town working in either shops or offices had had their lunch breaks and were just about to go back to work, and it was the usual place to go to get some last-minute business done. Hence, it was full. There was the full complement of three cashiers on duty, all working hard to settle their customers' business and send them happily on their way. But this was taking too long for me, and as I was the last in line, I decided it might be better to go to the health centre first and persuade someone there to complete that part of the Claim Pack that was relevant to them. This was another thirty-five minutes' walk, and, true to form, when I arrived, it too was full. My frustration was mounting. I looked around, and as I did so, a kind-looking lady seated behind a table selling raffle tickets told me to go to the dispenser at the reception desk, take a number and sit down. Eventually, I did as she asked. This was not easy, due to the sheer number of people who were there. I noticed that it was mostly elderly people who were sat down, with many other younger people standing in the aisles. I looked down at my ticket. It said:

Your number is: 24

Please watch the screen for your turn

I looked up and around for a screen and found it hovering, seemingly in mid-air, over the reception desk. To my horror, the number on it was: 79. My heart sank, and my frustration mounted further. How long was I going to be waiting here? The time was moving on. My plan had seemed so reasonable and simple to do, but then I had gone from the frying pan of the building society to the fire of the health centre! As I stood there with my brown envelope in one hand and my ticket in the other, I was sweating and breathing heavily and the number over the reception desk was not changing and no one was moving. It was awful! I decided to approach the desk. I was keenly aware that everyone present was watching me, probably resentful that I was pushing through, but then again maybe not, because if they were of said resentful mind, nobody stood in my way or shouted out their objection. I continued to push through. Ever so gradually, until I successfully arrived at the desk.

"Um, excuse me, please, but I don't really want to see a doctor, but someone from here has to fill out part of my form."

"I'm afraid you'll have to see a doctor. You cannot claim Sickness Benefit until your doctor has assessed you and signed your form," the receptionist answered.

"But I'm not making a claim for Sickness Benefit. The Job Centre told me that I had to bring this form here for a doctor to complete."

"But that is only if you are going to claim Sickness Benefit. This should have been explained to you, or you should have read about it in the information provided in your Claim Pack. If you are not claiming Sickness Benefit, I can assure you that you do not need to see a doctor." The lady at the desk was being very considerate, but my mind was so jammed with frustration and anxiety that it took some time for her answer to sink in. She waited a moment for me to answer, then said,

"Do you have an appointment, sir?"

"No, no, I'm sorry," I said.

"Then if you are not going to claim Sickness Benefit, and so do not need to see a doctor, or other health care professional, may I politely ask you to leave. As you can see, we are extremely busy."

"Yes, of course," I answered, and turned toward the exit and again, ever so gradually, made my way out through the crowded waiting room. By the time I was outside, it was really hot, and I knew that before I could deliver my form, I would have to go back to the building society. This meant another walk to Abergamlas and from there back again to the town centre. It was now three-thirty and I hadn't eaten a thing all day. But as I walked, all I kept in mind was that mine was a simple plan, and I would now demand the chance to tell someone at the Job Centre, and surely they would understand.

And so, on I walked. It was hard to pass my house, but I had to do just that. Eventually, I arrived at the building society, which, this time to my complete delight, was empty. This was such a relief! Mrs Cook greeted me pleasantly, but expressed some concern about me.

"Hello Mark, love," she said. "Are you all right? You look a bit peaky, that's all."

"The Job Centre has given me this form..."

"And you want us to sign it. Of course, dear. Let's take a look." I dutifully pushed my brown envelope under the glass at her desk. She then opened it and leafed through until she came to the part that was relevant to her. She looked away to the computer screen on her right and rattled the keyboard as she typed. When she stopped this, she picked up a pen and copied out on the form the details that she saw on her screen. This completed, she dipped a rubber stamp in her ink-pad and stamped the form. She read it through once more to be sure, put the form back in the envelope, and pushed it under the glass in my direction.

"There you are, then. And a word of advice to you," she said. "Post it and go home and forget about it."

"Not really thinking of that," I said, "I'd rather take it straight to the Job Centre."

"Yes, that's okay," she answered brightly. "Do that on Monday. Same thing."

"Monday?" I was puzzled.

"Yes, that's right. When they're open."

"Open? Aren't they open now? It's only half past four." That feeling of creeping desperation was working its way up my legs and into my thighs.

"It's Friday today, silly," she answered, smiling back. Fair play to Mrs Cook. She was always smiling. "They close at one o'clock on a Friday. Everyone knows that!"

"But I... But..." I trailed off, thinking of my financial situation.

"Tell you what I would do. I'd seal that envelope and put it through their letter box; it's only around the corner on the top of the square, and that would be the end of it. You'll hear from them in no time. Two, maybe three weeks at the most! You have nothing to worry about, Mark!"

She could see how I was feeling. There was no use hiding it. I was too tired and hungry. I would never be able to manage for two or three weeks. It was impossible without money. Then, Mrs. Cook's smile subsided as she watched me, and she glanced furtively at her computer screen, which I presumed still displayed my financial details, such as they were. She returned her gaze in my direction.

"Mark, come here, please, dear." Her voice was lower and more brusque in tone, suggesting that she was speaking to me on a different, more personal level, if you like. It took a couple of seconds for me to move, but as I approached her desk, she stooped underneath where she was sitting, and I could see that she was sorting some things out in her handbag. She straightened up, looking what was arguably serious for Mrs Cook.

"Mark, dear, please don't be embarrassed in any way, but take this and go buy yourself some food for the weekend." I looked down on her desk as she slid a £20 note under the glass. I stared at it in amazement for a while, and then looked up at her.

"Thank you," I replied, nervously. Slowly, I reached out with my right hand and picked up the money. I felt nervous and self-conscious, but I had no choice. My mind had become numb.

"First thing on Monday morning," she said, "go straight there and ask for an emergency payment. Tell them your situation and any plans that you have, and they're sure to understand. You may have to wait a while, but try and be patient and work with them."

I knew Mrs Cook was trying to help the very best that she could, but that horrible sense of desperation kept tickling its way up my legs and into my thighs and my groin like a sense of sick excitement. I struggled and struggled to leave. She had said something about telling the people at the Job Centre my plans, and this made me think about France, and about Argent Port de Bluff, and about Robert, who probably was wondering what had become of me and Vivvy, whom I couldn't help missing so much that it literally hurt, and about all the things we had left in our little room because we could not carry them. Robert had probably kept back our pay and tips, and it was all there waiting for me. All I needed was the ferry fare! Oh, why had I ever come back here! With the big brown envelope now looking ragged and torn, I gathered it up from Mrs. Cook's counter with her gift of £20. I tried to smile back at her. I think I actually succeeded because she smiled back at me. Amazing.

"That's right, Mark. Go home and have a cup of tea or something." Those words, simple though they were, seemed to do the trick. I nodded silently back and meekly opened the door of the building society and began the long walk home. Actually, it wasn't that far, but at the end of that particularly long, frustrating day, that's the way it felt to me.

Life on Benefits

That Monday morning, the Job Centre was crowded. I don't remember that weekend at all, but I remember I hardly spent any of Mrs Cook's £20, being extremely cautious as I had no idea at all about what my immediate financial future held. All I could think of was taking the accursed heavy brown envelope back to the Job Centre, walking all the way there. I had no money at all, and all my plans were on hold until the Claim Pack was in their hands. But at long last, here I was, in the Job Centre, waiting my turn, but not patiently. The reception counter was empty, so I stood there first, but after about ten minutes had passed, nobody came. There was no bell on the desk. I looked around at the clerks at positions 1, 2 and 3, but to no avail. To them I was invisible. It was so frustrating. Eventually, I knocked on the counter, and the man at position 3 nearest me, whose badge informed me that his name was Donald, looked in my direction. He was not pleased. Well, at least I have his attention, I thought.

"I've come to deliver my Claim Pack." I said pathetically.

"That's Admin," replied Donald. "Upstairs, first on the right." As he was busy writing something down on the paper in front of him, he pointed dismissively and absently with his left hand to the entrance. I walked away, following his direction. A sense of despair hung over me like a cloud. As I stood there, I looked in both directions and found the stairs to my left just inside the glass exit doors and began to climb. I felt as if I weighed a ton, but Esprit Fort kept telling me that this was good, and that all I had to do was hold it together for a little while longer and I would be back in France before I knew it. It struck me that he sounded exactly like Mrs Cook. Once I was at the top of the stairs, I walked to the end of the corridor and turned left, where the office entrances were. For some reason, I was surprised that there were offices on both sides. Clearly the building was much bigger than it looked from the outside. I felt very strange even being there, but having arrived at Admin, at least the end was in sight, I told myself. The door marked Admin was open. I did not want to make eye contact with anyone there, or to appear disrespectful, so I lowered my head, knocked on the door and waited.

"It's okay. You can come straight in. Everyone does." I looked up and a pretty-looking young woman, in a dark green business suit, whose badge informed me that her name was Linda, beckoned me inside with her right arm and then pointed at a fragile-looking, black tubular metal-framed chair placed on my side of her desk. I sat down with the utmost timidity, afraid it might not support my weight. It did, fortunately.

"Right then. What can I do for you?" asked Linda, brightly.

"I've come to deliver my Claim Pack."

It was all I could think of saying. It was all I wanted to do, then leave here and pay the ferry fare. *Come on*, said *Esprit Fort, not long now.* I nodded sullenly at Linda, trying my hardest to return her smile, and at long last handed the by now ragged brown envelope over to her. She took it in her perfect little hand and emptied its contents on the desk in front of her. Finding the main questionnaire, she turned each page as she speedily read through my answers, giving me the distinct impression that she had done this many times before. Then, once this was completed, she placed it apart to her left and surveyed the rest of the materials. I noticed that her facial expression had changed. Largely gone was her bright smile, replaced by a more serious, studied look, as if she was looking for something and was frustrated that she could not find it. She returned to my answer book and leafed through it again, this time more slowly. Then she stopped, clearly she had found what she was looking for. She took a breath and looked up at me, immediately the bright smile was back. Had she perfected this ability while practising in front of a mirror, I wondered.

"You don't have any signature from your doctor, Mister Bashford. I'm sorry, but we really need that."

My shoulders sagged, my heart sank and I felt sick and flushed. That horrible tickling tension returned to my legs and groin. I felt Esprit Fort grin an evil grin inside me. He was enjoying this.

"I went to the health centre," I was gasping for breath, "but the receptionist told me that if I was not claiming for sickness, I wouldn't need a doctor's signature. And besides, it was crowded and I was glad to get out..."

"Really, Mister Bashford." Linda raised a reassuring hand to bring me to a stop. "Really. Honestly, it's not impossible to deal with. Tell you what, if you sign a consent form, we can contact your doctor from here, but you have to understand that we need this, not because you're claiming Sickness Benefit, but because it's standard practice in our dealing with someone who has worked outside the country."

I suddenly felt like I was heading for a crash landing.

"But please don't worry," Linda continued. "All it takes is a phone call and your paperwork will be in the post to us the same day."

"But how long will all this take? I have no money at all and all I want to do is go back to France to my old job. Mrs Cook at the building society said that I could ask for an emergency payment – is that right?"

Linda's bright smile was gone. Thinking about it now, I feel quite guilty for robbing a pretty face of a bright smile, but right there and then, I had no time for such thoughts. I was desperate. Linda's look spoke to me of some real sympathy. Then she did that thing that all the others at that Job Centre did. Namely, wheeled back a couple of feet in her office chair, and searched under her desk. Strangely, this seemed to infuriate me. It was so frustrating. It was as if all the answers to my life lay outside my grasp, and only they had the access and the ability to grant them to me. I strained to hold Esprit Fort back from her. Eventually Linda straightened up and wheeled forward back to her desk, this time armed with a single piece of paper, which she placed neatly and carefully in front of her. On it, she did some writing on the "For Official Use Only" section and slid it over toward me. Then she swivelled the page clockwise so that I could read it and placed her pen on it.

"If you would sign it and print your full name, together with your National Insurance Number, you can take it downstairs to the reception desk, where they will arrange an emergency payment for you. You clearly have a very simple plan that should work out in no time at all. I do hope you're successful, Mister Bashford."

I did as Linda asked, thanked her sincerely for her help, returned her pen and left the room. Right then, neither Linda nor I had any idea of just how successful I was going to be, but that was because right then, whether I realised it or not, I can honestly not remember, I had hit rock bottom and would remain there for longer than I would care to think about, even right now, many years and a mountain of money later.

Twenty-four pounds and seventy-two pence!

It was as if my mind was jammed and the rest of the world was on mute. My head was spinning and I couldn't decide if the right thing to do was to try to keep calm or go into a flying rage. The truth is, both seemed like the right thing to do, and that was what made it worse.

Twenty-four pounds and seventy-two pence!

When I had walked into the Job Centre that morning, I had a plain and simple plan: and that was to go back to France to resume a job I loved in a place I loved among people I loved, and rent my house out. It was exactly what I wanted it to be. I knew what I wanted to do. I did not have to worry about paying rent myself because the house was legally mine after my parents died, so I did not need any rent allowance. I did everything they asked of me; I applied for job after job and then took all the rejection letters to them, and I did this in the vain hope that they would listen to me and my plan, but every time I tried to tell them, they explained rules about this, *and all in good time*, Mister Bashford, they said. All I needed was the fare for the ferry, but I didn't even have enough money to buy food for myself!

Twenty-four pounds and seventy-two pence!

This was the emergency payment. Following this, I would receive my full Unemployment Benefit cheque every fortnight. Do you have any idea what that was going to be?

Seventy-five pounds and thirty-six pence! Every two weeks!

Tell me, have you ever been on benefits? Do you think it's a slice of heaven? A permanent holiday? Money for nothing? That everyone on benefits is a bone-idle scrounger? Think again, dear reader! Because you're wrong! The mistake everyone makes is to assume that everyone on benefits is on them because they want to be. But again, you're wrong! Obviously, I cannot speak for every single person, but all the people I have met claimed benefits as the absolutely last resort, and then, they discover that it is by far and away easier and indeed enjoyable to hold a job down than it ever is to try to live on benefits. And that is certainly true of myself. I remembered what my father's philosophy of life was, and looked around again and again to see if I could possibly find something that everyone, or almost everyone maybe, wanted to be done. But the more I looked, the more tired and depressed I got. You see, that is the problem with benefits: they stick to you and they colour you and they seem to fill the air with glue. Once you're on them, there is no way out. I think they call it the poverty trap. I think it works like this: you get benefits, but when you apply for work, and go for a job interview, it's as if you've turned to stone in the eyes of your interviewer. I know. I've seen it too many times. Once they know you're on benefits, they don't want to know you! It's as if they think something like, Oh, he's all right – he's safe – probably likes it that way. I could see it in their faces! And another thing, and again with regards to myself, you will assume, as a reader, that, because of my age, and my name, that I have been an overnight success. But I assure you that that is simply not true either. Let me assure you, I had to do an awful lot of climbing before I could become the character that you think you know. By this time in my life, I felt that, through the travelling and the various other jobs that I had tried, that I had accrued some life experience, but, after my decision, my so-called quality decision, and with my fists clenched and my heart beating like a piledriver, I looked around in all directions on the front door-step of the house in which I had literally been born, and to my utter dismay, I could not tell which way to go or what on earth to do. I thought again of remortgaging my house to raise some money, but again I remembered again the crippling interest payments that I would have to make, and on a house that my father had paid cash for. No way! I would rather let it rot! People were also telling me how bad I was looking. I had become pale and thin, and walked about with both fists in my pockets, my shoulders slouched, and always looking down. Until I had actually been told this by a concerned neighbour, I had no idea that this was even happening. What was the matter with me? Surely I had mirrors in the house, but it's just something you don't see until you're told. To be fair, every now and then, one or other of my neighbours would invite me round and give me lunch. Well, you're one of us originals, Mark. Aren't many of us left, now, are there, hey? This was really very kind of them, but they eventually waned. I found more and more that I had to fend for myself. And this was only right, but my frustration was quickly getting close to boiling over. I wanted to scream at them in that awful Job Centre,

"Look, just stick your benefits!"

But I couldn't do that. As much as I wanted to, I just couldn't do that! There was literally nowhere else to go. There was not even the old Co-Op butchers anymore, or even their new up-coming competitors. The only butchers now were in a big supermarket about half a mile outside the village on the new land development. And then, don't forget, there was the effect of the slow process of the way that benefits kill your soul; humiliation. From going in there in the first place and telling them your situation and the black moment when they give you the so-called "Claim Pack", everything changes. Nothing about it even remotely sets you up to be in the least bit optimistic about finding anything like a job, or better prospects. But what else could I do? Well, if you know anything about me, you know perfectly well what I did. And yes, it was a really, really stupid thing to do, and there was absolutely no justification for it and I promise NEVER to do it again. And do you know what? I'm in my sixties, now, and I haven't done it again yet!

What can I say here about it? If you are one of the majority of the human race who has never committed a crime, and well done you, by the way, you will be understandably unaware that committing a crime is not something you rationally decide to do. It's not as if you sit down one morning and, after a hearty breakfast, objectively and casually weigh up the pros and cons in the light of an article in the morning paper! The world is a very distorted place when you're desperate.

And I was desperate.

After about nine weeks of living like this, life had become totally meaningless. Everything and everyone and every moment is the same, dull, boring grey. Then, slowly moving like a vast and bloated slug, the monotony built and built gradually every day, until one afternoon, that *fateful* afternoon, I found myself outside at the bottom of the garden of my house, attempting to sort out some things in Hawkey's old shed with tears rolling down my face as I thought of him. Trying to get my mind off how depressed I was, I had sorted out some of his old tools, putting the ones that had gone rusty to one side, while all the better ones, I put into a box, hoping, *intending*, to sell them at a local auction. Perhaps then I would be able to raise enough money for the ferry. I wouldn't have worried about getting to the ferry itself by train. I would gladly have walked the forty-five miles to the port. Then there were some odd-looking blocks of wood. I hadn't noticed them until right then. I had no idea what they were or why they were even there, but as I started to sort them out one by one, my only thought was how much money I would be able to raise. There was an old chair, and I took it outside into the garden and sat on it and continued, not even noticing that it was a beautiful day. Then I turned this one particular piece of wood over in my hands and something completely abstract about it stuck me. It was L-shaped, from a piece of old furniture I had never seen, but it looked to me in my then altered state exactly like a gun. After

I had whittled it into shape with my Dad's old whittling knife, a skill lost today because of the ban on carrying knives, I got up and went back into the shed and found some cardboard boxes which I knew were under the workbench that contained some rusty tins of paint. I found some black paint and painted my piece of wood. I had not done a very good job, because my hands were trembling, but if you've ever been in the position where you have to make up your mind to either pay the bills or buy food to eat, you'll understand that I simply didn't care anymore. I was very glad that the paint didn't take very long to dry due to the heat of the day, and so, now, armed, *of a fashion*, I put it in my pocket, walked in the old familiar straight line through the doors of my parents' home, out of my front door for what was not quite the last time, turned left, and walked towards the High Street, not caring what would happen next.

My destination? The building society.

The Abyss: From Benefits To Prison

I was silently escorted to my cell and sat down on the narrow steel bed to woefully begin reflecting on my utter stupidity, and of course, equally woefully, to begin my sentence. I was told not to worry, to keep my head down, to stay the hell out of trouble and that I would be out in far less than the six months that was handed to me. After all, mine wasn't exactly the crime of the century. Actually, it was a six month sentence suspended to four months, but what did that mean when you are staring at it from the beginning? To be fair to all the prison staff, they were very concerned about me. They knew all about me, and that what I had done was more stupid than malicious, but a price had to be paid and I had to be made to understand the idea of real consequences. But my sentence was too harsh. Although it merited nothing more than a period of Community Service. Yet there was no denying it; here I was, in an actual prison cell with other actual prisoners. The guard promised me that first night that he and his colleagues would go easy on me until the day that I stepped out of line. This prospect filled me with terror. I shuddered at the thought of what not going easy on me meant, and the question of what did he mean by stepping out of line. I guessed in that respect if I *were* to step out of line, it would be something I would know at the time. But surely, it would be too late, then. And how would *stepping out of line* affect my sentence? None of these thoughts were helping me, but the worst one was that it was what I deserved. My fears were large and not about to go away, but the largest monster in my head by far was despair. And its closest friend was loneliness. I was my parents' only son, and just in case I have not already mentioned it, both my parents were only children too. So I was literally on my own.

I lay down on my bed and settled down for what I simply knew was going to be a sleepless night. I can clearly remember that the process of decline which had resulted in my not caring about consequences suddenly stopped right there. I don't know what it was. Maybe it was one thing in particular, like the sound, or the smell, which was clean, by the way – very clean. It smelled as if it had been cleaned right at that very moment. It made me feel, as I closed my eyes, as if I was in hospital rather than in prison. But no, it was not that. It was the whole experience and knowledge of where I was, and with that the sure knowledge that what I did from now on mattered, and mattered a lot. One way or another, my life was never going to be the same again.

No, there was going to be no sleep tonight.

Then I fell into a dream. I was still awake, but I was in a dream as well. I went back to the day when I walked away from my parents' house towards the High Street. That was not its real name. That was Jones Street, but we called it High Street because that was where the handful of surviving businesses could be found. It was where the old Co-Op shops had been, but not anymore. There was instead, a Mini-Market, a betting office, a Newsagent, a post office, a small bank and the building society. My father had always favoured the building society rather than the bank, because they were more friendly and tended not to ask as many questions. The banks were for the toffs, he said.

I was definitely not a master criminal or anything. I was at the end of my rope, and that's all there was to it. I did not burst in and shout. I very quietly opened the door, instantly aware of the chime of the bell above it as I entered, and again as I closed the door behind me. It had once been a corner shop, and the bell was one of the shop's original features, but the building society kept it as a memento of sorts. I thought that it was a very sedate, pleasant and polite atmosphere and I felt a strong pang of both regret, perhaps even self-pity, as I took my piece of painted wood out of my pocket. Mrs Cook behind the counter, smiled at me.

"Oh hello, Mark. How are you, dear?" It was then that I remembered that I had not paid her back for her kind help. I obviously felt really bad. It felt like I was falling into a void, but there was no way out and there was for me definitely no way back. I placed the piece of wood on the counter, pointing it in her direction. In the glaring light of this former corner shop, it was obvious it was not a gun. I felt supremely stupid. She straightened up and smiled back at me in a sympathetic, very disarming way before I could say anything.

"Now come on, love. Calm down and go home. Everybody knows you're not your best these days, what with being out of work and all. I know it can't be easy for you."

Then Mr Walker, the Branch Manager, came out from behind the counter. "Yes, lad. Jackie is right," he said. "Just go home. There's no money here for you." These people had known me since I was a child. They had known both my parents. Mr Walker was a cashier, an office junior, you might say, the day my father had brought me here to open a savings account. I stared at them both silently, trembling and on the verge of tears, darting my gaze left right left right. I was shaking uncontrollably. Then I felt tears starting, but something caught my eye to make me look round.

Flashing blue lights.

The police had arrived. I was instantly angry with them both, but they insisted then and in court, later, that they did not call the police. They had the situation under control. It was nothing, really, they said. Mark was about to go home, they said. They would all have put the whole silly business of a moment's stupidity behind them for good. They would, that is, had it not been for the passer-by who saw what was happening through the window from outside, and rushed for the nearest phone box. The truth is that what happened changed the course of my life. One way or another, life could never be the same after it. All I had to do was make double sure it got better not worse, but I was absolutely not in any way optimistic on that subject. Having seen too many prison dramas, I convinced myself that even staying out of trouble would be a job that would test the utmost strength of any man.

But I was unaware at the time that I already had a dark, brooding guardian angel, someone who, on my very first night, was watching me very closely. So closely, in fact, to even take an interest as to whether or not I drifted into sleep.

The First-Timer

That first night seemed to have a very strange effect on me. I was very surprised at how quiet it was. I don't know what I had been expecting, but there was nothing but silence, sometimes broken either by quiet footfalls in the corridor outside my cell, or a guard talking quietly to a colleague or one of the other inmates. That was another thing that impressed itself on me. We were never called prisoners, only inmates. The whole thing had left me feeling totally numb, both mentally and emotionally.

The truth is I was so frightened I had no idea what to do next.

But guidance came from two directions: the official direction, and the unofficial direction. So far, I had not spoken to a single other inmate. Not even to ask a name. In the morning, I was told to go get a shave and a shower and be in the mess hall at seven sharp. No excuses.

"How can I have a shave?" I asked, when I arrived. The guard wordlessly handed me a razor and a towel.

"The towel is yours, but you return the razor to the guard at the showers after you've finished. Don't try to be clever and hold on to it. Trust me, there'll be hell to pay. Just hand it over. Easiest way all round, lad."

"Okay," I answered meekly, and walked past him to the showers. From what I had seen in the French prison movies with Vivvy, I was terrified of going anywhere near the showers, but there was simply no alternative. And besides, I genuinely needed to feel clean. I was very relieved to see two guards outside, but all they did was to stare at me as I walked in. There were only two other inmates present. I thought this was strange. I was expecting the place to be crowded. I showered and shaved in silence, came back out, and made sure I handed the precious razor back to the guard on my left, who obligingly directed me to the mess hall. I had no idea what to expect in terms of a mess hall. But it turned out, in my mind at least, to be no more than a canteen. Again, I was dreading whatever passed for a meal, but was once more relieved to see and glad to say that it was not only good but enjoyable, also. No one really spoke. We ate our breakfast of bacon, eggs, fried bread, hash browns, sausages, beans and mushrooms with either a mug of tea or coffee, again, in silence. My mind was a whirlpool of thoughts about what lay ahead and how I was going to deal with all this, when, directly to my left, there was another inmate sitting on the same bench next to me. He had sidled up as silently as the morning, and sat there equally so. I carried on eating out of a mixture of hunger and fear, although to be truthful, he didn't look all that intimidating, but then again, I guessed that it was nothing to go by.

"All right, then?" he said, without looking at me. "First-timer? Must be shittin' yourself. Word of advice, son. Keep your nose clean, don't ask for no favours. And I mean none at all. Always be aware of who's watchin' ya. At the moment, it's the guards what's watchin' ya, but they won't always be, see. Don't get me wrong or nuthin' – the guards are always watchin', but they won't always be watchin' ya like they are now, see. Suicide watch, they call it, see. Just makin' sure you don't top yourself or nuthin', see. But after them, it's either the pervs or the lifers. If you ask me, you're better off under a lifer, 'cause you know where you are with them. Nuthin' to lose and they've done it all, see. I guess you might say that I'm on a sort of errand from one of 'em. And that's doin' you an' me a big favour at the same time, 'cause you don't wanna get caught by one of the pervs, mate. Bad news, that. Well, see ya round, then, eh? You got the speech next. First-timers always get the speech on their first day. Governor always waits for the first mornin' to give 'em the speech." And with that, he was gone. As it happens, he was wrong about seeing me around. Whoever he was, I never saw him again. I finished my breakfast, and followed the other first-timers. And as I walked, I thought.

Two thoughts would not let me go: the first one was that for the whole time that I was in prison, there was the memory of that fateful day at the building society. What a stupid, stupid thing to do! What on the face of this green earth was I thinking? And worse than that, there was that moment when I was sat outside my father's shed, on a beautiful day, when I looked at a piece of wood, thinking it looked like a gun! Why would I possibly think that? And how did that idea even begin to resemble anything like a solution to my problem at all? And what *was* the problem? All it was, that I was in a temporary situation of being out of work, which would have been put right in a short time with the next job that came along. In fact, all I really had to do was go back up the road in the other direction to The Sun Inn and ask them for my old job back. Simple! Yes. Simple! Now! From inside a prison! Hail retrospect, the saviour of us all! It was my inability to think straight that put that accursed Claim Pack in my hands, then allowing it to fill me with a false hope of being a solution that had landed me in all this trouble now. True, my sentence was a short one, given as a message to society at large and myself in particular that this kind of behaviour would not be tolerated. Okay. Message received. By me at least. Can I go home now, please? The plain answer to that one was:

Not just yet, lad.

The second thought that overstayed its welcome in my head was the more immediate question of what my temporary dining partner had said with regard to being watched. The suicide idea was simply an observation area. That was pretty straightforward and made perfect sense, and not at all worry-worthy. But far more worry-worthy was the thought of who *else* was watching me, and was the present tranquillity to be explained only by the being on suicide watch? By now, a sense of despair was not the only thing growing inside me – it was now great pals with terror!

Presently, we arrived at an office door. Impressively engraved on the frosted glass was: *G P Barnett Chief Prison Officer.*

One of the two guards walking with myself and the five other inmates knocked on this door. The unseen voice from behind it invited us to come in. We obediently marched into the office, and at the order of the other guard were told to line up and stand straight, which order we, of course, obeyed. MrG. P.

Barnett, a pale, overweight man in a brown suit that looked like it should have been discarded ages ago, sat behind his desk and silently inspected us. He gave a barely audible cough, removed his glasses and, remaining seated, began.

"Good morning, gentlemen. I do hope you enjoyed your breakfasts. I am assuming that you are now all ready for the challenges of what lies ahead, so let us proceed, shall we? If you have even the thinnest slice of common sense, you will have by now come to the conclusion that you have all hit rock bottom. All your collective criminal acts, greater or lesser, it matters not in the slightest anymore, did not work. This was because your stupidity was not merely illegal or even criminal. No, it was quite simply wrong. I'm not a bleeding heart liberal, and so what I say is this." At which point, he decided that it was the right moment to stand up. I suspected that this was a well rehearsed move for him.

"Even though at one point in your lives you may have thought that you were on the up-and-up, the truth now is, that you are buried so far down in deep shit that the light of day has been long lost to you, perhaps regrettably long before you ever landed in my office this morning. And if you are ever going to make it back out into that precious state which the common man takes for granted, and more importantly than that, if you are going to stay out and continue enjoying staying out, here, right here and now, as you stand on this very spot, is where you take the first step to start climbing. Make no mistake, everything, your life in here and outside, and the lives of your friends and families, hang on what you decide at this precise moment. I promise you, that if you play ball with us, we will definitely play ball with you. But I equally promise you that if you decide that you are smarter than the rest and that your time in here is only a temporary interruption to your fledgling careers as criminals, we will make very sure that we do not play ball with you or that you play ball with anyone else. Such behaviour will not be tolerated. We are here to make sure you pay your debt to society, but during that time, you can turn it into an opportunity to make yourselves ready for the outside world, successful and never to return here or anywhere like this ever again. I trust that you will think seriously about these things. Once again, good morning, gentlemen. You are dismissed." As he returned to his desk, the first guard ordered us to turn right and leave the room.

So that was The Speech. Pretty good, I thought, but my self-esteem was at an all-time low. As if The Speech was not enough, we were then assigned our respective jobs. We had to do these and stick to them. No complaining. All the other things, like study time, job-seeking and career advice, would be decided by how well we did these jobs.

But, to my surprise, we were not taken to our jobs. I did not even know what my job was.

We were taken, instead, to the Remand Room. The Remand Room resembled what I would describe as an old-fashioned school reading room. Two of its walls were covered by bookshelves. There were not many books on these shelves, and it appeared that whoever had put them there had not cared very much what they were, whether women's romance paperbacks, guidebooks or advice pamphlets. They lay there in disorganised little piles. We were told to sit at the desks at the centre of this room, and fill out the forms that would be handed to us. We were asked if we wanted something to drink, either tea or coffee, these were on the table in the corner. My tension ever so slightly subsided. I fetched my cup of tea and went to the opposite corner and sat down. Two of the others who had been led here were talking very loudly, boasting that this was going to be a doddle and more like a five-star hotel than a prison! Outside world? Keep it, they said. I sank down behind my desk and drank my tea in silence, taking care not to look up, but to fix my stare straight ahead. I was appalled. They had clearly taken no notice at all of anything they had just been told.

Eventually, an officer entered the room and all of us, the two boasters included, sat down. The officer looked around the room, silently inspecting us in the same way that Mr Barnett had previously done, and when he had satisfied himself that all was well, he gave us each a questionnaire of stapled white A4 pages and a black ball-point pen which had to be returned at the end of this session at all costs. We were asked to complete our forms, not leaving a single page blank, and to answer each question honestly and truthfully. Extra paper would be supplied if we needed to continue further. The more we said, the better, we were told. Please also carefully read each page, and make sure you follow all the instructions.

I looked down and started to read. I was being asked, firstly, to provide all my personal information, and then, secondly, to explain my crime. There were many, many questions asked about it, from the obvious ones about my motives and the reasons, to other, seemingly unrelated ones about family, friends and work colleagues. What did I think the effect of my crime would have on them? There were even questions about my sex life! After having read the so-called instructions, I raised my head furtively and stared up to my left at the room's only window. It had bars on it and it was dirty, but I saw that it was a beautiful day outside, and I knew that I was not going to experience any of it. I sighed.

Jobs, Jobs, And More Jobs

Being told our jobs was a long time in coming. They had been allocated, we were told, but our induction was not yet complete. A week may not seem a long time to you, or for that matter to me at my present time of life, but back then, in that highly lamentable situation, it seemed like a year. Despair had set in. I was asked to complete form after form, explaining myself repeatedly, and attending interviews and counselling sessions. This happened day after day for a whole week. At certain other points during this time, we received medical examinations; the worst of these was intimate and invasive. That it was strictly supervised was no consolation. I had developed a faraway stare.

Eventually, they decided with regard to myself that as I had worked as a waiter, they placed me in the kitchen. I had never worked in a kitchen, I tried to explain, but they took no notice. True, I could cook, but I did not consider myself skilled in that area at all. I had no idea what they wanted me to do, or who else, or how many other inmates had been assigned the same job – whatever this was. I was, for the first time since I had been admitted to prison, genuinely feeling both curious and enthusiastic about this mysterious job that I had yet to start. After the boredom and misery of a week in the Remand Room, I really wanted to do something that at last resembled a reason to be awake in the day, and something that was different to sitting in a chair and filling in forms, together with all the other demeaning things we were put through. I feel, after many years of reflection, that it had all been part of the dehumanising process; a way of getting us in line and making double sure we didn't step out of that line in any way.

Just what would I be doing?

It did not take long before the mystery was finally revealed. It was all the things done in a kitchen that did not involve cooking, and none of them pleasant. At least, considering the sheer scale of operations conducted in a prison kitchen, to say nothing of the conditions and the breakneck speed in which I was expected to move and complete each of my given tasks, it was not like anything you can imagine. It was not as if I was sat by a mountain of potatoes with a bucket of water by my side and a potato peeler in my hand. Oh, no! There was a high-standing machine that was large enough to take a whole bag of potatoes in one go. You did this by emptying said bag into the opening at the top, clamping down the lid, turned the tap on, switched on the machine, let it rumble for a while, then turn off the tap, switch off the machine and open the big heavy door in the front ready to catch the freshly machine-peeled potatoes in a huge plastic bin as they came cascading out. You gave these to the cooks, who instantly ordered me to stand away. This was because they poured them into the chip-slicing machine. At no time was I ever allowed to go anywhere near a knife, or any machine that contained a blade. After finishing all that, and it took most of the morning, the rubbish had to be emptied. This task was, in my opinion, among the worst. The area around the potato machine stank of stale and dirty water. But rubbish duty meant that I had to put heavy bins of food waste onto trolleys and wheel them outside to the loading bay at the back, then turn ninety degrees and drag them up the slope, pull the brake lever, and pour them into the waiting swill silo below. On the one hand, it was the only breath of cool air I had from the stifling heat of the kitchen, but on the other hand the gut-wrenching stink that assaulted me as I opened the silo was unbelievable. As I took the first bin in hand, I realised to my horror that I had to take a deep breath to lift it. The very foulness of the air around the silo was so strong I could taste it. I waited until my stomach had stopped retching and I had enough breath. Then I heaved the huge plastic bin onto the rail above the silo. As it rested on the bar, it began to bend, and I had to act quickly or I would lose my grip, so I slowly lowered it back onto the trolley. I caught my breath again, again breathing in the foul smell of the silo as it wafted upwards toward me, and tried a second time. This time I was a little too successful. The lower half of the bin landed on the silo bar, almost dragging me with it over into the silo myself! But thankfully the heavy, filthy, slimy contents of the bin emptied in one huge plop, splattering into the silo in no time at all. Phew! But my relief was short-lived. There was another bin the same size on the trolley, and another eight more waiting in the kitchen, and that obviously meant four more trips just like this one! Then, as if that was bad enough, after finishing these trips up and down this slope, I was then consigned to the pot room. This was full to the door with the big pots that were used for the cooking. There was no time to lose, because in about half an hour, the preparation would begin for the next meal, whatever that was. By now, I couldn't care less. But the first thing to strike me about the pot room, and taught me to dread it, was the heat. I kid you not, the pot room made the rest of the already cauldron-like kitchen actually feel cool by comparison. With no choice in the matter, I set to work. I scrubbed with all my might, heavy pot after heavy pot, slamming them face-down onto the enormous draining board. As I scrubbed, I longed for rest, but none was to come. I was too tired to think about anything. I just kept on scrubbing. I was sweating uncontrollably. It seemed as if there was no end to it. At one point it looked like there were not many left, only to find that even more had been dumped inside the door. I was sinking further in despair. This was serious. Then, the kitchen seemed to fall silent. At first, I thought I was imagining it, but I went to the door, and most of the staff were gone. What was more, there were only two more pots left. Seeing the light at the end, as it were, I rallied, and finished the two remaining pots. Convinced that these were the last of the day, I headed towards the lockers, but as I did so, was stopped by a cook, who stood with his arms folded. He gave me a nasty look.

"Where the fuck do you think you're going, then, hey?" he scoffed. "What do you think this is? Half day? Get the floors scrubbed! The only people who can tell you to go are the guards, and have any one of them said anything to you about leaving? No! So what do you think that means? It means you're here until. Got it? Good! Now scrub the fucking floor!" And he stormed off. I felt as if I was drowning. He was, of course, right. I had completely forgotten about the floor. And even the guards, for that matter. Then I looked at the kitchen as a whole, as if seeing it for the first time. I discovered that it was an enormous place! Wearily, I looked around for a mop, or whatever it was that was used. It was then that I realised that I was the only inmate in the kitchen. My despair turned into worry as to what this meant, and the reason for it. But I dismissed the thought, I had to. I was too exhausted to do or even think about anything. Eventually I found a deck brush and a metal bucket and started to work. The work seemed never-ending, but this was a kitchen that served up hundreds of meals every day. I wondered if there was anything corrupt going on here, but they worked me so hard that I soon lost all interest. Eventually, I saw even the idea of thinking independently itself as a luxury. As I scrubbed, I thought of my parents' house. My home since birth. It was empty, now. Its simple comfort denied to me. Instead I was here suffering all this. I tried to think of what I might be doing if I was not here, but my mind was blank. I simply carried on scrubbing the floor, staring into space but seeing nothing. There was no light at the end of the tunnel. There wasn't even a tunnel. There was nothing.

All I could do was scrub the floor. I started in the middle and worked my way around in a clockwise direction. It was the only way I could think of to be sure that I was not going over the same place twice. But life is not as simple as that. As soon as I would allow myself to think that I had completed one area, a cook from another area would call me over and get me to clean their area. I also noticed with growing foreboding that the bins were filling up, and I knew only too well what that meant! Surely, I thought in my weakness, it would have been more in line with common sense to empty the bins, wash them out and then scrub the floor. But nothing was done this way, and if I tried to suggest otherwise, I was answered with a tidal wave of verbal violence. Eventually, I surrendered myself to silence. Just to carry on scrubbing was my only choice. Another thing I noticed was that the only break I had all day was my lunch and evening meal. Yes, I was in that heat for the whole of the day. There was no relenting. Knowing and thus fearing the way the cooks behaved towards me, I dared not ask about study time, or anything else outside this, this... whatever it was! All that seemed a world away from the one I was currently living in. Not only did there seem, but there was in fact, no escape from this drudgery. It was never-ending. Even when at last the day eventually ended, I was denied a shower, to be told that access was only granted to inmates of my category in the mornings. I was exhausted and covered in sweat and then, to make matters even worse, I had to go to bed without being allowed to take a shower!

As miserable, sweaty, filth-filled day followed miserable, sweaty, filth-filled day, I felt I had hit the bottom of the pit of despair. I exchanged my overalls for a t-shirt and denim shorts. My steel toe-capped boots were stolen from me, and because they were too expensive to replace, I had to make do with a cheap pair of training shoes. These were definitely the wrong things to have on my feet for a kitchen of this size. The kitchen floor was solid Victorian-built stone, and it was always greasy, even after it had been scrubbed. This meant that staying on my feet was something I always needed to think about. But I was not always successful. I frequently slipped and fell, landing hard. Very soon, I was covered in bruises. I lost far too much weight, due to exhaustion, heat and over-work. I met every day with a morbid, despairing feeling of fatalism and misery. As I looked in the mirror every morning as I shaved, I noticed that my face looked as if it had somehow sunk. I became convinced that I would not survive.

The routine was always the same:

- alarm bell rang
- get up
- take towel
- walk to shower
- collect razor
- enter shower room
- shower and have shave
- return razor
- go to kitchen.

And that was it. Welcome to my world!

The Levee Breaks.

By now, I simply carried out all my tasks as if I was sleep-walking. I didn't think what to do first. I just did it. I honestly don't know how long I was like this. It seemed like forever. I found the bin trolley and heaved the first two heavy bins onto it. It was early in the morning and it was unusual that they were already full, and the kitchen itself was stifling hot. Normally it took a while for these conditions to develop, but obviously not today. As I normally did, I put all my weight behind the trolley and pushed. I turned a corner when a cook stopped me by standing directly in my path. He stood there, legs apart and arms folded. I knew better now than to ask what he wanted. I stared submissively down at the floor, waiting for him to speak. I trembled with a combination of fear and tiredness.

"Leave that. The vegetable shed wants cleaning. Follow me."

I left the trolley behind and followed him. I was both surprised and glad that he had not been abusive or threatening, but I knew by now that in spite of his manner, it would have been wrong and perhaps dangerous for me to expect him to be a friend. I simply followed him to the vegetable shed.

"We're 'avin' a new delivery this mornin' and it needs to be cleaned out. Grab a bin and empty the shed of everything, yes everything, and scrub the shed clean as soon as." And he simply walked away, leaving me to it. The *shed,* as such, was itself an indoor building. I had faintly hoped that it might provide me with an opportunity to have some fresh air, but sadly this was not the case. The only bucket I could find was the metal bucket I used for scrubbing the floors. This meant that I had to fetch it from the other side of the kitchen, from where I dragged it clattering along to the vegetable shed. Once I had arrived, I let go of it and opened the shed door. The overwhelming smell that rushed out at me made me vomit. It was filthy. It was crawling with flies and maggots and rotten vegetables, and this time I knew I would have to put my hands in it! The only meal I had eaten that day had been breakfast. I had no idea of the time, or when or even if I would have anything else. Nor did I care. Now, all thought or relish for food had gone completely. The swill silo had been bad enough, but this? This was the worst so far! I looked for an empty bin to set to work, but of course there were none. This meant another trip to the silo. I walked back to the other side of the kitchen once again to find the bin trolley. It was exactly where I had left it, except that, as they were on the trolley to be taken to the silo, they were now overflowing, with the trolley being treated as a bin in itself. With my stomach still dancing around to be sick again, I pushed the trolley once more the rest of the way to the silo. When I eventually returned to the shed, two of the cooks, the two that had previously laughed at me when I opened the shed door, now stood watching as I slopped the rotten, heavy filth into the bins. In the back of my mind was the horror of returning yet again to the swill silo to empty them, but first things first, I thought. Eventually, the shed was empty.

I stood outside the shed for a moment coughing and retching, not even daring to put my hand to my mouth to cough because both my hands smelled as bad as the shed! When I stood upright, I saw a hosepipe rolled up on a hook on the wall just outside. I unravelled it and turned the tap on, turning the water first on my filthy hands. It was ice cold and sent a refreshing shiver through my whole body, conveying with it a message that perhaps, just perhaps, there was light at the end of this tunnel. I hosed down the walls and the floor, aiming to sweep everything away towards the drain just outside the shed. Then a loud klaxon noise sounded and one of the cooks came up to me.

"Time for lunch, mate," he said. He was one of the younger cooks. He cracked half a smile. "If you think you're up to eating, that is." I sighed.

"I'll try." I said wearily. He laughed.

"You'll get used to it. Don't worry. Go wash your hands and get some grub."

I instantly and eagerly obeyed.

I stared in the mirror again when I was in the toilets, and was surprised to see how dirty my face was and that my hands were dirty again so quickly. And on the subject of quickly, I was also vaguely surprised at how quickly the morning had gone. When, after I had washed my face and hands, I joined the line in the canteen, something began to dawn on me. I had no idea what the time was. I had got into the habit of looking down, so if there had been a clock on the wall, I would not have seen it. I asked the boy in front of me.

He turned around and spat in my face.

"What do you wanna know for, then, Mister Lardy-da! Got an appointment, have you! Someone important you want to meet? Not in here, mate!" The boy behind me pushed me forward at him. The spitter grabbed my shirt in both fists and growled liked a dog.

"See, it's like this, see. Time don't mean a fuckin' thing in here. All you do is what you're told when you're told to do it. Now piss off and wait your turn like everybody else!" He let me go by pushing me back at the boy behind me who had first pushed me forward. I tried to steady myself in case I did not hit him again. This was ridiculous. Everything was becoming increasingly meaningless. Yet the spitter was right. Time had no meaning in here. When the court had sentenced me to six months, although I was devastated, at the same time I also thought that it was not that long. But here, now, feeling like this, I knew that it would be a lot longer than it seemed to be. I blankly picked up my meal and sat down, ate it without even looking at it or caring what it was. It could have been anything. I quite literally did not care. I drank my mug of tea, got up, returned the tray to the trolley and went back to the kitchen. I remembered what Mr Barnett, the Chief Officer, had said in his office as we had lined up in front of him. He was right. I had hit rock bottom. My despair felt complete.

I walked around the corner to the door marked "Kitchen Staff Only" back into the kitchen with my shoulders slouched, staring at the floor, neither inclined nor even daring to look up. The cook who stood in my way as I entered was less than pleased. He hit me hard in the middle of my chest with the heel of his right hand, forcing me back a couple of steps to stay on my feet.

"What's this?" he shouted. I looked up.

"What? Uh, what do you mean?" I stammered. I had no idea in the world who he was or what he could be talking about. He hit me again in the same way.

"No! No! Don't try to come the innocent with me, you bone idle bastard! Have you seen my shed? It's fucking filthy! And you swan off to lunch and leave it just like that without no by or leave? Is that what you think you can do? Well you're wrong, mate. I'll show you!" He grabbed me by the shoulder, spun me round and forced my left arm right up behind my back and frogmarched me all the way over to the shed. I honestly thought he had broken my arm. When we were there, he shoved me forward, onto the bin. I thought I would be okay, but the momentum was too much. I went crashing into the bin, the bin toppled over, spilling its foul contents on the floor, and I went after it, landing in a sodden pile of rotten vegetables. But this was not enough for him! He kicked the mess on the floor into my face and then made another kick, a savage one right square in my ribs, and I almost fainted with the impact. I was sure he had broken something. The pain was unbearable. The wind had been knocked out of me, and I couldn't breathe. I struggled around in the mess franticly trying to breathe, but he kicked me in the same place again. In an attempt to hopefully prevent another kick, I lay still in the filth. It seemed to work. He seemed satisfied now that the second one had done the trick and he leaned forward. I was shaking, with pain, weakness and the effort it took to breathe. I knew that I had swallowed some of the slime from the rotten veg, and it was stinging the back of my throat.

"Now get the fuck on with it! And in future, I don't care if it's lunchtime or high tea or whatever the fuck! I don't care if you've got visitors, or even if it's the fucking Queen! If you're doing a job for me, you fucking finish it first! Understood?"

I nodded, but this made him worse. He kicked me in the ribs for a third time.

"Don't just fucking nod! Answer me, you wanker!"

"Yes. I understand." I blubbered in the slime. Then at last I heard him walk away. I cannot describe the relief I felt, even though I was in the worst state I had ever been in my life. This was worse than anything I could have been afraid of.

I was seriously injured and I knew it. I wanted to cry out with the pain, but now that I was on my own, I was more concerned with getting to my feet. I had to try. But try as I would, this was impossible. I definitely did not want that cook, whoever he was, coming back. The last thing I wanted was to give him any chance to beat me up again. I tried again, but I was too weak from my injuries. I fell flat on my face, face down in the filth I was lying in.

"Help me, please!" I cried out pitifully. I sounded so pathetic to myself. Then, with that, an unseen hand grabbed the back of my t-shirt and pulled me up, and another hand grabbed the back of my shorts. I was being moved. I was so grateful! I didn't care who they were; I was just glad someone had heard my cry for help. I was lifted up and the sense of relief was too much for me. I cried out loud like a baby.

"Thank you! Thank you so much!" I sobbed.

"Ha ha! Aw, that's all right, sweetie. Don't you worry, now! It's nice and comfortable where you're goin'!" And they both laughed. I was suddenly bug-eyed with horror again. The trip was a short one. To the inside of the vegetable shed!

"You sure about this?" the one at the back said.

"Definitely," the other at my neck answered. "Buck tenderised 'im for us. Amazin' that. Considering he's the veg cook and all!" They both laughed again. But they were in a big hurry. The perv holding my collar kicked open the shed door. Once inside, they both set about kicking me in the ribs to make sure I wouldn't resist. And I didn't. I had lost all hope. I didn't kick about or struggle or resist in any way. They did what they wanted. Both of them. I was too weak and injured and in too much pain to fight back and they knew it. It was this very thing that I had dreaded while I was being detained in police custody, but it was to be far worse than I imagined it to be, now that it was actually happening. I wanted to scream and be sick at the same time, and I certainly wanted to fight back, especially when they were fumbling around with my shorts, trying to pull them off. The trouble for them was that the filth that still remained on the floor of the shed and outside it was slippery and I was covered with it, and so it was difficult for these two sick bastards to remove any of my clothing. I remember thinking that, if I was able to fight back, this would be the best time to kick seven kinds of stuffing out of them, when a crashing blow to the back of my head knocked me clean out.

Waking Up In Heaven?

I woke up in a hospital bed. Everything was clean and silent and pure. I was not in a ward; I was in a room by myself. I could not think straight, but because it was so peaceful all I could think of was the sheer beauty of the absence of danger, and that prison was or had to be, over. I started to cry. The sound I made, such as it was, alerted the duty nurse. He came rushing in.

"Well, hello there, sleepy head!" He put his hand on my forehead and then looked for my right hand. When he lifted it, I saw that three of my fingers and my thumb were in plaster. He held my wrist ever so gently and felt my pulse for a couple of seconds, then equally gently replaced my hand and quickly studied the information displaying itself on the machine on the wall behind me. He smiled.

"Good to see you. Your temperature and pulse seem okay, considering you've been out for three days."

"Three days!" I croaked, as loudly as I could manage.

"Oh, don't worry about that, silly. That would be the painkillers. You had to rest. I'll go and see if the doctor is available. I'm sure he'll be glad to see *you*. Before I go, open your mouth for me, would you, please?"

I obeyed, and he swabbed the inside of my mouth with a lemon flavoured refresher. To me right then, its sweetness was beautiful. I was obviously "Nil By Mouth", probably as a safety measure. His talk had helped me feel better, but I was having trouble getting my head around it all. All my efforts in trying to speak to the nurse had left me exhausted. I was obviously too weak. I also noticed that I was not moving about. I felt nothing, either physically or emotionally. I had been so busy thinking this way that I had not noticed that the doctor was standing to my right. Luckily, he had been talking to the male nurse that had greeted me. When the nurse saw that I was taking notice of them, he touched the doctor on the arm and pointed at me. Instantly, he turned in my direction and they both smiled at me. I managed a smile back. The doctor, although he was quite young, had a surprisingly senior voice.

"Mr Bashford. Hello at last. I am Doctor Sepand Kavarana. Nurse Mills has been keeping a very careful watch over you. Do you want me to continue talking with you? Your injuries, compounded by your weakness, are in my opinion considerable. If you do not wish me to talk to you, please do not be worried at all."

I nodded as best I could, hoping that by doing so, I would be telling him that I definitely did want him to continue talking with me. He turned to his left and faced Nurse Mills, who looked me over carefully, and then gave a single nod.

"Okay, but just for a short while. Early days, yet." the nurse said.

"Very well." answered Doctor Kavarana. "But while I will proceed with the utmost caution, I must also speak very frankly with you. Your injuries are as follows, Mister Bashford. You have suffered three fractured ribs, a ruptured spleen, and..." he trailed off, and lowered his head as if to look at his shoes. I braced myself for what he was going to say. He made a light fist, placed it at his mouth, gave a gentle cough and took a deep breath. "And a pierced anal wall. I am so sorry. You will have our best treatment, and when you are ready, prison staff will visit you and speak with you. I will also tell you that there is a guard outside this room. You are very weak. The reason you are not in any pain at the present moment is because you are being administered very powerful painkillers. I will keep doing this either for a couple of days or until you are a little stronger. And at a time when I and Nurse Mills think appropriate, this will gradually stop and we will get you out of bed. I have to warn you that the road back to full mobility is going to be a very hard one. But I will leave you now to get some rest. In the morning, we will see if you can eat something. It is quite late at night now, so you will be better off getting more rest. I give you my very best wishes for a full recovery. Goodbye for now, Mister Bashford." He took the clipboard from the nurse, leafed through a page or two, then handed it back and left the room, leaving the nurse standing alone. He smiled at me and shrugged his shoulders.

"Don't worry. They're all the same. I have to leave too, but I won't be long, okay?"

I weakly nodded my understanding, put my head back on the pillow and, before I had time to digest what the good doctor had said, was fast asleep.

Welcome To The Comfort Zone

All I knew was that I was in a whole different world and that I was thoroughly enjoying it. Yes, I had heard all the terrible things that the doctor had said, but right there and then I felt that I was floating happily and contentedly adrift on the crest of a wave in an ocean of pure comfort. The beautiful painkillers continued to faithfully administer themselves, sending me sailing away, surrounded by a womb-like serenity. All thoughts that this was artificial, or that it would be hell trying to get back on my feet and strong again didn't even register. No, here for once at last I felt as if I had landed in Paradise itself. No more pervs. No more prison. Peace at last.

This most blissful of states seemed to go on and on for days and days. Nurse Mills monitored me, bathed me, changed me and fed me. Maybe I should have counted the number of times he did these things, but I did not. If I had been so inclined, it would have been because I was not content, and was anxious and keen to be back on my feet as soon as possible, but that's just it. I was the exact opposite of all these things. I can truthfully say that I did not want it to end. And to be fair, I felt that I had a right to enjoy this after all that I had been through, and this painkiller induced state was the best way of forgetting all about it. It was a highly memorable time for me. I remain convinced that whatever this medication was, if they put it in the water supply, there would be world peace overnight!

It was beautiful.

Then, one morning, Nurse Mills came in, this time alone, to conduct his normal monitoring of my condition. But I had the vague impression that something was different. For one thing, there was no smile or greeting of any kind. He reached straight for the machine behind me, which after all the time I had been in that room, up until that moment, remained unseen by me. It bleeped as it always did when he did that. Then he went to the foot of my bed and picked up the clipboard that was hanging on the rail there, made some notes and replaced it. Then, and only then, he stood still, straightened himself and turned to face me. But this time, and for the first time, his expression was serious.

"Mark, I have to tell you something, okay?"

I braced myself for I didn't know what.

"We've been gradually reducing your medication in very small steps every day until today. But before I say anything else, let me ask you how you are feeling."

"I don't know." I said quietly.

Nurse Mills rushed to my side and put his left hand on my right shoulder. "We can't go on giving these to you or you'll never be able to recover, and I'm sure you don't want that, do you?" He squeezed my shoulder encouragingly. "Come on. It'll be okay. The dose is a lot lower than you think, so stepping off the boat will be all the easier. Besides, it's not as if we're going to make you run a marathon yet. We'll give you a couple of days first!" He winked at me and smiled. I knew that he had succeeded, and he in turn could see that I was okay with it. I tried to regulate my breathing. I swallowed. I even tried to smile back at him.

"Okay. Is it lunchtime yet?" I asked, trying my best to sound cocky.

"Let's see what they can rustle up down in the kitchen, shall we?" he winked.

"Never mind, never mind!" I answered, much louder than I thought I was able, any flirtation with levity stopping right there with me at the mention of the word kitchen. The nurse stopped still in the doorframe with a very worried look on his face.

"Listen," he whispered. I wondered why he was whispering all of a sudden. "Don't forget who's outside that door." The penny dropped. "I'm so sorry. Believe me. Let me go and see what I can get, okay?"

I nodded. His smile returned. He left the room and I fell asleep again. The painkillers had plainly not worn off.

An Official Visit

"Good afternoon, Mark. How are you, lad?" asked Mr G. P Barnett, none other than the Prison Manager himself. I noticed that he was wearing the same crumpled brown suit. He was accompanied by a uniformed prison officer whose serious appearance at least gave me the impression that he was of a high rank. They both shook hands with me and seated themselves comfortably. They had been told that they did not have long, and to bring that message home to them, Nurse Mills had insisted on being present.

"I suppose I'm doing my best, sir. Thank you." I smiled courteously at him. Still, I couldn't help feeling nervous, wondering what all this was about.

"Well, take your time and make a good job of it is what I say." said Mr Barnett. He sounded as if he were quoting from a book. "Recovery is never an easy or quick business."

"They are taking very good care of me here, sir," I replied.

Mr Barnett nodded his head and took on a very serious expression. He coughed deliberately, to clear his throat and rally his thoughts.

"That's all very well and good, but we've come here today to do two things. Namely, to ask you about what happened to you and to bring you up to date with some news about your situation. Is that all right with you, Mark? We didn't want to do this too soon. That's why we've waited until now. I can tell you that some of the news is good, but not all."

I was immediately curious about what this news would be, especially if some of it was good, and I was certainly willing to answer some questions first in order to get to that. I guessed he was using a carrot-and-stick technique of sorts. I looked towards Nurse Mills. He nodded.

"Yes, okay." I answered.

"Thank you, Mark. But please excuse my ignorance. Allow me to introduce you to Officer Anthony Taylor."

"Call me Tony." Tony was a tall, well-built man of few words, whose square-jawed face did not lose its serious expression even when he was, as I assumed at that moment, trying to be informal. I sensed a latent rage present in him, but on reflection, I guessed it was about my situation, rather than myself in particular. Mr Barnett continued.

"Well, Tony is now responsible for putting together all the information about what happened to you for the purpose of presenting it as a report to the police. We understand that the police will also want to speak to you as well." He held up his hand to Nurse Mills. "But that will of course only be when the hospital thinks you're able. And not until then."

I nodded silently back. I was growing impatient. I just wished he would get to the news!

"To begin with, what can you tell us about what happened?" asked Tony.

"All I remember, sir, is that the chef dragged me over to the vegetable shed and beat me up just outside. And then, when I was still on the floor in the muck, the two pervs came and carried me into the shed and raped me."

Nurse Mills stepped forward, frowning at them.

"Who were the pervs?" asked Tony, taking no notice.

"I don't know. I was face down in the muck. I'd been sick. I couldn't see who they were." Tony's face twisted in a scowl of frustration. Then something else flashed in my mind. My eyes widened.

"Oh yes! One of the pervs said that the chef was called Buck." Tony's reaction to this was an actual laugh.

"Buck? Are you sure?"

"Yes, sir. I mean, Tony. Sorry." Tony closed his eyes and shook his head to indicate that there was no problem, and turned to Mr Barnett.

"You know who he's talking about, don't you? Matthew Buck. Got a record himself. GBH. And guess what for?" Tony chuckled. "Queer bashing. Can you imagine? Goes to show, doesn't it?" Mr Barnett's face was wide-eyed with amazement. Tony turned back to me.

"Are you sure there's nothing else you can remember?"

"No. Nothing, I'm sorry. I was knocked out cold."

"Knocked out? As in unconscious? Yes, you were in a mess and all, but you were moving about on the floor in the shed mumbling stuff nobody could understand. I ought to know. You were reported missing and I was the one who found you."

"I'm sorry. I don't remember any of that. All I know was that I was hit on the head and then I woke up in this bed three days later." I was getting really tired now, but at the same time, I was afraid that Nurse Mills would notice this and step in at any moment and stop the visit, which I was desperate that he would not, because I wanted to know what this news was. I could feel myself sweating and my sense of frustration rising. Mr Barnett raised his left hand to Tony and turned to face me.

"This conveniently brings us to the other reason for our visit. And I must take this opportunity to thank you, Nurse, for your patience."

"You haven't got much longer, judging by Mark's condition. So if you could bring things to a finish, please." Nurse Mills sounded like it was all business. Clearly he was in no mood to do any comforting.

"Ahem. Yes of course, Nurse." answered Mr Barnett, "we will oblige." He faced me again. "Well, Mark, you may be aware that the Prison Service has a legal office accessible to both staff and inmates. On review, there has been a growing opinion that in your case, your sentence was overly severe and that a non-custodial option would have been more appropriate. Unfortunately, our most earnest appeals to have your sentence either terminated or reduced have been unsuccessful. Once you leave this hospital, I'm afraid you will have to return to prison for the remainder of your sentence. There are, however, several mitigating factors involved in this. Firstly, your period of recovery here will be counted as part of your sentence. That is why a guard has been posted outside this door, in order for there to be a prison representative present. Secondly, when you do return to prison, I have taken the measure of completely removing you from any labour and transferring you to our new Study Unit, where you can choose a course of education which would in your case be continued after you leave custody, together with help and advice in seeking employment. You will be given every assistance in this. Also, in a less official capacity, shall we say, you will have the protection of a fellow inmate. The gentleman concerned is one Ellis Nathaniel Robbins. I can entrust you to him with the utmost confidence, as he has been instrumental in the help of many other inmates, as I am equally sure he will be with you. And finally, I am confident that you will be delighted to know that it has been decided that you can be compensated for all that you have suffered whilst in custody. We as prison staff contend that your sentence has been excessively gratuitous, and although we sadly in lost our appeal on your behalf for a termination of your sentence, we have nevertheless succeeded in gaining for you a promise of compensation, on the basis of being a victim of violence. Unfortunately, it is not very much, at twenty thousand pounds, but it is still a sizeable sum and should be of some help, at least, in helping you back to a normal life. I sincerely wish you every success, Mark."

And after that lengthy, and still after all this time, perfectly remembered speech, Officer Tony and Mr G. P. Barnett stood up, and each wearing their own personal interpretations of a smile, gently shook hands with me again in as formal a way as possible for someone lying in bed, said goodbye, and left my room.

After they had been silently escorted out, Nurse Mills was stood facing me in the doorframe.

"Sh! Sh!" he shouted as he darted his head back and forth between my direction and the corridor until he must have been dizzy. He was waiting impatiently until Mr Barnett and macho officer Tony had entered the lift. Then his eyes brightened when he saw that they were gone, his face lit up with a big smile and he came running into the room to me.

"Mark! Oh, I'm so pleased for you!"

"I'm going back to France! I've got my life back..." I trailed off. "Thank you, Nurse Mills. You're a good man, and..."

"Andrew. No, sorry, Andy. Please! If it's okay to call a tough guy like him Tony, Andy is okay with me!" He had both his hands on my shoulders. I thought he was going to kiss me. "Aw, Mark! If anyone deserved this, you do!

I couldn't help it, but I was totally overcome with emotion about it, too. Perhaps it was Andy's emotion rubbing off on me. I don't know.

"Ahem!" Andy said loudly.

"What? What!" I said, now in a state of confusion.

I hadn't noticed it immediately, but Andy had stepped back to draw my attention. I had drifted into thinking that I would do the few remaining repairs to the house first before I took the ferry, and what they might be again after all this time away.

"What? What!" he mimicked cheerfully. "Well I hate to be a party pooper, especially at a time like this, but don't you think there's something else you have to do first? Hm?"

"Yes, I know," I sighed. "I have to go back to that prison."

"Well yes, there may be that. We're not sure, are we?" Andy replied, "But I was thinking of something more, you know, immediate." He pursed his lips and waved his hand in front of me and pointed with both index fingers at the floor as if he was directing traffic. The penny dropped. An alarm went off in my head.

"I've got to get out of this bed, Andy!" I gasped.

Breakfast

Breakfast has for some reason always been my favourite meal of the day. It has a lot going for it in my book: you know, being the first meal of the day, and all. Besides, it seems to me to be the only meal I really look forward to, with its wide array of unpretentious content making it fun to eat as much as anything. I woke up after my best night's sleep since being completely off painkillers. Andy quite rightly suggested that it was the reception of the good news from serious Mister Barnett and macho Tony, as he called them, that did the trick. I agreed. Once I was washed and freshly dressed, Andy stood straight, and up close to me with his hands behind his back, looking to me as if he were almost standing to attention. I was hungry and felt mildly disturbed. I wondered if there was something wrong.

"This morning is special, right?" he said. "You're going to be taking your first steps for a long time, right? So, I wanted to make an occasion of this, and so what I've done is... just wait a moment!" He raised his right hand and pointed upwards with his index finger and ran to the door of the room, and from out of my sight behind the wall in the corridor, he wheeled in nothing less than a silver trolley. I was absolutely amazed. Breakfast with all the trimmings!

"Breakfast is served!" he shouted, triumphantly, and we both laughed. One thing was for sure – I was certainly motivated to get back on my feet! I at once realised that this was not the usual run-of-the-mill hospital breakfast. I knew that he had paid for this himself. I sighed.

"Thank you, Andy," I said. "Seriously, you shouldn't have."

"It was my pleasure," he replied, brightly. "I sneaked the trolley from the doctors' lounge. They don't half live it up, those doctors, don't they?"

"They deserve it all and more still," I said.

"Oh, and one more thing!" Andy said, again quite loudly. "If you're going to put your feet on the floor this morning, you're going to need these," and produced a gift-wrapped parcel from behind his back.

"Thank you," I replied. I was lost for words and stunned by his generosity. I tucked in to my delicious breakfast, finishing it with what was to me at that time a gourmet coffee, and opened my gift. It was a pair of denim slippers. Seeing them conveyed to me how serious this morning really was. It may not have been a giant step for mankind as a whole, but it certainly was for me! Andy had left me lost in thought as he silently cleared my bed tray, wiped it clean and took the trolley back to the doctors' lounge. And that was the exact moment, after he had left my room, when I realised how much I wanted to walk again, and to be free again, but just how far away that freedom lay, I was then mercifully, gift or no gift, unaware.

The Uphill Gravel Road To Recovery

"You should have waited! You fool!"

Andy was horror-struck at what he saw on his return. I was sweating, crying and lying in a pool of my own urine on the hard floor, bruised and in pain from my failed attempt to get out of bed. I couldn't even get my new slippers on!

"Paul! Can you come in here, please? Quickly!" he called to the guard directly outside my door. The guard came rushing in.

"You grab one arm and I'll grab the other and we'll get him back in bed, shall we?"

I was not very heavy at that time, and so picking me up and putting me in bed was an easy job for them. I was not critical of the guard for not coming in the room to my aid, because Mr Barnett had clearly explained that his presence was purely as a prison representative. But still, some unofficial common sense would not have gone amiss, I think. When I was back on the bed, I was trembling, upset and in pain.

"Honestly, Mark. What were you thinking?" Andy said in his soothing voice.

"I just wanted to get out of bed!" I wailed. "But I didn't even get as far as putting my new slippers on!"

"Look, nothing is broken, okay. But you are hurt, so we are going to have to cancel your mountaineering appointment for this week, if that's all right!"

"Mountaineering?" I cried, "I might just as well have been told, right mate, if you're going to get back on your feet, all you have to do is to jump over the Grand Canyon at a single bound! That's just as impossible to do as put on these slippers myself!"

"Listen!" Andy shouted firmly, calling me back to reality. "Never mind all that for today. Let's get you clean again and relaxed, and then we can think about what to do next. And I do mean 'we'. Is that clear, Mister Bashford?"

I nodded meekly, but a worm of discontent slithered around inside my stomach, and was turning into anger. Esprit Fort was watching me from a distance. I held him back, even though he felt very powerful, feeding on my desire for freedom and independence. Andy's face was full of sympathy and concern. There were definitely many other things he wanted to say, but he nodded to the guard, who nodded back and silently returned to his post just outside my door. I watched him leave and I couldn't stand it anymore. I tore at my urine-stained robe and flung it away from me and looked down at my thin and bruised body. I had obviously not even recovered from the beating both outside and inside that terrible vegetable shed. I wept loudly.

"Look at me, Andy! Just look at me! I look more like a victim of famine, never mind violence!" and wept and wailed again.

"You're going to get better, trust me!" he answered in his most earnest tone. I had too much respect for him to openly contradict him, even though I was at the lowest point at that time in my life, but let's just say that I felt a certain credibility gap between what he was saying and the empirical evidence of my present state of health. I had to face it. Full recovery, let alone freedom and independence was a lot further away than I thought.

The following morning was far less ceremonial. A simple wash and brush-up, followed by my medication, which was in turn followed by breakfast. This time it was standard hospital-issue, but with one odd difference. Before he served it, Andy placed a plastic cup with a plastic spoon and a paper handkerchief on the table over my lap in front of me.

"I want you to eat this first, please, Mark," he said firmly.

"What is it?" I asked.

"It's a food supplement. It's to try to put some weight on you. We'll give it a couple of weeks, then see how you are. Doctor's orders."

"What? No breakfast?" I answered, hopefully a little light-heartedly. His strict manner was beginning to get to me. Thankfully, he chuckled. Well, it's a start to a more pleasant atmosphere, I thought.

"No. It's not a food substitute. It's something you eat before your meal. You'll have one before every meal. Listen, the doctor will see you soon. He wants to monitor your progress for himself." He tapped me on the shoulder. "And not a word about the trolley, or I'm in trouble!" His smile had returned, and that meant things were all right. I was glad. Andy was a good man, and I had acted foolishly and he was justly upset. I was resolved to make sure that it didn't happen again. Prison had definitely taught me that good people are precious, and that it was all too easy to upset them. And once they're gone, they're gone. I smiled back.

"Thanks, mate. Don't worry. From now on, you're the boss, trust me!" I looked at the plastic cup on my table.

"What flavour is that? Do you know?" I think I must have felt some of my father's steel rising in me. Andy shook his head.

"I don't know," he gave a quiet chuckle. "Does it matter?"

"I don't really think so, but my mind's made up, now, Andy. I'm thinking that I would rather be in prison and on my feet, than in hospital and in bed. What's more, it'll show the pervs that I'm not afraid of them. That I haven't swung it so that I'll be in here until my release."

"Oh that's it! You've got rocks in your head. Definitely!" he whispered loudly. He didn't want to shout in case Paul, the guard outside the door, would think we were arguing. "I'm no expert on things like this, but I would soundly guess that anybody who was in prison would give their right arm to be in your place. They'd pull a right old fast one, and no one would blame them! Stay put, that's my advice. Especially after what you've been through!"

I sighed. He was, of course, right. I picked up the plastic cup off my table and took off the lid. Inside was a dollop of pink goo. If it looked awful, that was overshadowed by its horrible sickly chemical smell. I placed the lid on my table, picked up the spoon, ate the pink goo, wiped my mouth with the paper handkerchief, returned both it and the now empty plastic cup to my table and lay back. Andy had sat and watched this whole thing. I looked at him and gave a token grimace, though it didn't really bother me.

"Just to confirm. That was not a pleasant experience." We both laughed. It was good. "One way or the other, let's make a deal, both of us. Let's get me out of here." We shook hands and cheered to that.

"But after yesterday, we have to make sure you're strong enough," said Andy.

On that, we were definitely agreed. Breakfast followed.

More Visitors

Time passed, during which I was given many meals and equally numerous cups of pink goo. The day-to-day monotony of it left me bored rigid, but it was all part of my recovery, so I stayed with it, never once complaining, even though that was all I wanted to do for most of the time. After a few more nervous and horrifyingly painful attempts to stand, I eventually succeeded. Andy told me it was progress. I smiled weakly and agreed, but it was far too slow for *my* liking. It seemed that the more so-called progress I made, the more frustrated I got. But it was a marked improvement from my former despair. Andy was a great encouragement to me, and kept repeating that he was pleased that at last I could stand. I smiled again. Maybe not so weakly that next time. He was, of course, winning me over.

I also had two visitors in relatively quick succession, each of whom came alone. The first was macho Tony, who had come to give me an early warning that the police would soon come to question me after his now completed report had been handed over to them. He also told me that he and his fellow officers, under the supervision of the Prison Manager, Mr Barnett, were now for the second time going through the same legal channels to question the validity of my sentence. He said that it was important that they did this again, because even though they had not succeeded the first time, this renewed application would be compounded by the fact that the police were now involved, and thus build a case for higher compensation and possibly even the earlier termination of my sentence, which they were all of the firm conviction I highly deserved. It would also serve the future good in the case of any other inmates who could be helped in a similar way to myself. He told me he was glad to see me putting weight back on. I was delighted to hear him say it. This was the first indication from someone who was not a health care professional that I was making some progress in this area. He was genuinely pleased when I told him that, although I could not walk properly as yet, I could confidently stand.

"In that case, it won't be long before you *can* walk," he said, but still without changing his serious expression.

Eventually, after a little informal conversation, which came as a pleasant surprise to me, we both stood up and shook hands, properly this time; he remarked that the plaster on my wrist had at last been removed. Another small indication of progress. He patted me encouragingly on the shoulder, and left.

Some days later, exactly how long I cannot tell, he returned. His consistently serious expression made him difficult to read. Was he going to contradict himself, I wondered. And what about the compensation? He seated himself comfortably, and once again complimented me on how much better I looked. I thanked him and said no more. Just get on with it, will you, I thought but dared not say. Eventually, he did say.

"Mark, I feel that you are owed an apology. All is going

well with our appeal on your behalf, but there is a certain fall-out that you should be aware of. All the legal proceedings are conducted in open session. This means that the general public are free to attend and sit in on any or all of them." He paused. "And that includes the media. On our way out of the building, we were completely surprised to be fielding a barrage of questions from them."

I looked around the room, but Andy was away. He was spending less time with me lately. I was of the opinion that this was to encourage me to think and act more independently. We had managed to get to the place where I was no longer afraid of taking a few steps with the aid of a walking frame, but this information coming to me now was new. I found myself spiralling into that horrible feeling of unfamiliarity.

"What's going to happen to me, sir?" I asked, trying to hold down a feeling of rising panic.

"Nothing you need worry yourself about, lad," he said.

"Yes, sir. Of course. Thank you."

He stood up and handed me some paperwork, and asked me to sign my consent for the continuation of their work on my behalf, as it was going further than it had on their first application. Of course I did this, and he again shook hands with me. But I noticed that there was no pat on my shoulder this time. Then, without another word, he turned and left me alone with my thoughts. We all know that good news travels, but bad news travels faster. It was at that moment that I noticed that there was no television in my room. So news of any kind, as slow or fast as it may travel, could not reach me. Maybe this was part of my custody; I don't know. This had been of no importance to me until now. I finally complained to Paul, the guard outside my room, about this in the light of Mr Barnett's previous statement that I should be allowed access to newspapers and other reading materials. He promised me that he would make all the appropriate enquiries through all the appropriate channels when he was given the chance. I sighed. This would only mean more waiting. I wondered just how many people knew about me, and what effect this would have on my life.

However, it didn't take very long to be allowed to have newspapers and a book to read. This was such a relief. Also, Andy told me that it would help with the healing process, because I finally had something to occupy my mind. This helped the day along, and my general mood improved with it. I took to it like a duck to water.

Then one day, there was a babble of very animated conversation in the corridor outside my door. I was immediately curious, as this was something that never happened. I knew it was not the doctor, because Andy would have been very much in attendance in and around my room, telling me all the preparations I had to make. I did wonder if it was the police, who had yet to visit me. But it was not them, either.

You can imagine my surprise, then, when it was none other than Mrs Cook from the building society who entered. I was sitting now in the armchair that had recently been brought in as an encouragement for me to change my position. Andy had placed it beside my bed on that particular day. I was busily and happily scanning through the "Situations Vacant" column in one of my newly acquired newspapers, trying to think ahead.

If I was told I had a visitor and was asked to guess who, Mrs Cook would have been my last guess! I pressed both hands down hard on each arm of the chair to raise myself up and looked around for the walking frame, but before I could even make a start, Mrs Cook embraced me warmly as if I were a long-lost friend.

"Mark! Mark! Are you all right, love? I tried to visit you three times, but I failed. We were all so worried about you! Then, with the news about you on TV..."

"TV?" I said, genuinely alarmed. "What do you mean?"

"What, didn't you know? Of course! You couldn't have, being here."

"What did they say?" I asked again.

"Well, they showed your picture from the court case." She sat down in a visitor's chair. "Terrible thing, that was! Everybody in the town thinks so, don't you worry about that! Well, the reporter said that your sentence was so severe that even the prison was making an appeal against it. Good thing too, if you ask me. They said that provided you were kept safe, there was no need to worry, but then, when you were attacked! I'm so sorry for you! I do hope you'll be all right! You know that what you did was very silly, but to go and get attacked and everything into the bargain. You certainly don't deserve that, now, do you! We didn't want to press charges, you know. It was Head Office that did that. But as you know, we all stood up for you in court, didn't we?"

I nodded. I had tried to speak a couple of times, but I knew that she was on a roll. I didn't want to offend her for the world. I knew that everything that she was saying was true and correct. What I did not expect was the television coverage. When macho Tony had told me that there had been media attention, I thought that this would amount to nothing more than a short article in the local paper. But this!

"Listen, let me tell you something I don't think you know," said Mrs Cook, bringing me sharply out of my reverie. "My husband is the local Justice of the Peace!" She paused, perhaps so that her surprise statement would have time to sink in for emphasis, or maybe even for dramatic effect. "He'll find out when that hearing is, and try and put in a character reference for you. Don't worry. The whole town will be there when we find out when!"

"All I can do is say a big thank you, Mrs Cook," I said, eventually. I had, of course, no way of telling how much influence the good Mr Cook JP could exert, if any, but I concluded that if he felt that he could do some little thing, and if that little thing, whatever it was, helped me, I could only agree. Mrs Cook smiled sympathetically at me, gave me the box of chocolates that she admitted she had almost forgotten about, hugged me once again for good measure and assured me that I would see her again. Please understand me that this was something I really appreciated.

If I'm honest, I didn't know for sure what my state of health was. I was able to get out of bed, yes, and was now even able to use the bathroom that was next to my room without any help, but walking any distance with confidence, indeed, without a walking frame as young as I then was, remained a level as yet unattained. As all these thoughts crowded in on me, the thought that I was being paraded across the media was not something that would go away. As I dozed uneasily in my chair, the local paper on my lap fell to the floor. All I wondered was, what in the wide world will happen next?

Eventually, I had reached a state of mind which could

reasonably be described as happy, or at least contented.

A little.

And what new dizzy height had I gained? Yes, I was now at long last able to walk around the very limited area of my room. In the face of all my previous failed efforts, Andy was reduced to insisting sharply that the sooner I mastered the art of walking independently, the sooner I was able to defiantly walk out of this room, fat cheque in hand, into the rest of my life without as much as a backward glance.

But yet strangely, I felt in no rush at all to get through these exercises. I took an average of two hours to complete them. That's right, two hours! Then, at a point when I felt that I had done them justice, I would lie down again, *recovering* from my recovery! Then, as soon as I was able, I would go to the bathroom next door and take a shower. Then, soon after this, without fail, the trolley lady would come with a choice of tea and coffee and biscuits and chocolate bars. And as if by way of perfect timing, a man from the newsagents on the ground floor of the hospital would come with a selection of newspapers, magazines and paperback books. I especially appreciated this, as it had been firmly forbidden to me until very recently. I snatched up a national and a local paper, together with a travel magazine and a careers leaflet. I was sat in my chair when Andy visited. He busied himself with the charts on the clipboard hanging on the rail at the foot of my bed, deliberately taking his time to look up at me with an expression of obvious mock seriousness.

"And how is the patient this morning?"

"As well as can be expected in the circumstances, thank

you, Nurse," I answered in like manner. There was a moment's silence.

"I think you're far better since the lady from your home town came to see you. You seem more willing to give the fitness for freedom thing a try. In fact, you're really trying your hardest lately." He tapped me on the shoulder. "Well done!" Then he finally gave in and smiled broadly. I found it most reassuring and encouraging. My eyes widened, suddenly remembering. "What's the matter now?" Andy asked.

"The papers!" I said, reaching for them and ruffling the pages loudly trying to find any trace of my *story*! "Nothing!"

"What? Are you afraid you're falling in the ratings or something?" Andy laughed. "Besides, you shouldn't be thinking about that. You should be just taking it easy until you can walk away from all this. Never mind the papers!"

I stared at Andy silently for what seemed to me an age. It was as if I was looking into the future, and Andy was still there. I drank my coffee. It was delicious.

"I think this a key moment for me, Andy," I said, feeling very time-out-of-mind.

"Really? How so?"

"Well, I think this is the most content I've felt for a long time and I didn't even know it." Andy's smile wilted a little, and then, after a pause, returned.

"All I for one will say to you is; well done and keep it up!" He leaned forward. "But take your time," he whispered conspiratorially, and left the room.

I lazily continued to read my papers and magazines, and dozed. I suppose it was my acceptance of what Andy had said that finally did it. Yes, Andy, I thought, I will take my time.

Yes, for the moment, I was content here. I had been told by the Prison Manager himself, who had taken the trouble to personally come to see me and tell me expressly that my time in this room counted towards my sentence. I smiled. I sighed. Contented.

Hello, Mr Bashford

"Hello, Mr Bashford. What is your preference today?" The man at the trolley asked me. I looked down at the row of newspapers and chose only my usual national, there being no new local paper. I paid him the token I had been given as my allowance, thanked him and waited for him to leave.

But he did not.

"Are you all right in here, Mr Bashford?" he asked me. I shrugged.

"I suppose so." I conceded. "Not much choice really."

"Yeah, but I suppose it's better than prison, right?"

I nodded. He rearranged the papers on his trolley. But still he did not leave. I felt sure Paul, the guard at the door, would order him to leave, but he did not.

"Still, can't be that long to go now, though, right?"

I made a funny face and shrugged for emphasis. I waited. He fell silent for a short while.

"And what about the money? That'll be good when you get it, no mistake I'm sure."

I backed away, instinctively.

"Paul! Please ask this man to leave." I didn't have to shout as he was stood outside my door right next to him.

"Come on, mate," I heard him say. "You're getting on my nerves, too. Hop it."

"Come on, Mr Bashford! Haven't you got anything to

say?"

The penny dropped. I knew who this man was, or rather, I knew *what* this man was.

The press!

Paul guessed this too, now. And without another word, took hold of the trolley with one hand and pulled it away from him aggressively. As he did so, there was a loud crack on the tiled floor. We all looked to see what it was. We searched around and it was the Paul who spotted the voice recorder. Before the reporter could get to it, he picked it up and snapped it with both hands and slammed it down on the trolley.

"Hey! That sort of thing doesn't come cheap, you know!"

"Don't care, mate. Now take your trolley and get out and crawl back under your stone!"

"Okay! Okay! No problem! Just wanted to ask a couple of questions, you know! Freedom of the press and all that!" He took hold of his trolley and scrambled off down the corridor towards the exit.

As soon as he had gone, everything was quiet again. Forgetting that I was pleased that I had walked as far as the newspaper trolley, I remained standing still. I had the newspaper in my right hand, but then I realised that I was clutching it in a vice-like grip and was grinding my teeth. I must have been making some sound or other, because Paul looked into my room to make sure I was all right. It was obvious that he was not pleased with what he saw.

"Wait a minute, there!" he said, looking panic-stricken. He held out his right arm toward me, waving with his hand, gesturing me to calm down. He glanced down the hallway to his left. "Nurse!" Then he snapped back in my direction. "Listen, mate," he said, shakily. I couldn't understand what had him so spooked, but I said nothing. All I knew was that I felt angry and my stomach felt as if it was tied up in a knot. But I wasn't angry with him or Andy, or anyone else for that matter. Just that reporter. I wanted to tell him that, but for some reason, the words just would not come.

"The nurse. Your friend. Will be here in a moment, okay? Listen to me," he looked around in both directions as if he were about to cross the road. "Don't mess this up. You haven't got long to go. If you play your cards right, you'll be out of here before you know it! You might even get to spend the rest of your time from here!"

I already knew this. What was wrong with him? And why was I so silent? Then Andy came in. He was out of breath and had obviously been rushing to get here. I was glad to see him.

"Come on, Mark," he said soothingly. He placed a reassuring hand on my shoulder. He nodded to the guard who returned a glance that said he was not convinced and moved himself back only a pace or two so that he could still see me, but not far from his normal position. Andy walked me away from the door.

"Let's get you back to bed for a while, shall we?" he said.

"Bed? I don't understand. Why?" It was all very strange.

"Never mind that," he said, and nodded again to Paul. "There's nothing to worry about, and besides, it would be a good idea to get some rest for a while anyway. Wouldn't it?"

"What's wrong, Andy? It's me. I'm okay." I felt relieved that I had finally got around to saying something.

"Well, if you're okay, you'll be a whole lot better again for some rest. You need to calm down. I can give you something to help, but it's better if I don't. It'll show that you can do it for yourself, you know?"

I laid back on the bed, feeling more confused, now, than angry. Andy drew closer to me and glanced furtively at the door. When he spoke to me, it was in a tone of voice only a little louder than a whisper.

"Listen. When Paul popped his head around the door, he thought you were going to attack him. Yes! Yes!" he said, putting an index finger to his mouth, wordlessly telling me to keep quiet, "I know that's not what you were going to do, but that's what it looked like, and when I came in, that's exactly what I thought was going to happen. For the first time since you've been here, Mark, I was afraid of you."

He sat me down on my bed and stepped back a pace. Then he took both my hands and put them on my lap. He smiled, convinced that I really was okay again. To make double sure that he knew I understood, I smiled back. He continued in the same whisper tone.

"I know it must feel terrible, but it looks like there's light at the end if you'll give it a chance, and it's not that long to go. You'll be back in France before you know it!"

All that he said was true. And I felt better for hearing it. I laughed. Yes, I actually laughed. Andy turned towards the door.

"It's safe to come in, now!" he said to Paul in his normal voice. "Everything is back to normal." He laughed as well. Paul walked back into my room and took a good, long look at me, then took a breath and sniffed.

"Had me going for a minute, there, I'll tell you that for not much."

"Very sorry about that," I said. "Won't happen again. Promise you that. But I was only angry at that reporter, that's all. Just hope there's no more of that to come."

"Course not," he answered, jovially. "Just a flash in the pan. It'll all be forgotten about soon enough. Don't you worry, mate. Put your feet up. Tomorrow they're bringing in a telly. Won't know yourself then! It'll be a big help for you to bide your time, too. You won't be bothered by the press ever again, I'm sure." And we all agreed. Eventually, Paul and Andy left my room. I drank from the glass that Andy had left, closed my eyes and drifted away.

Waking Up In Another World

I woke up feeling lazy and comfortable. I took a long, slow, deep breath and gave Vivvy a gentle cuddle. She smelled like warm toast first thing in the morning. She moved and murmured something wordless and turned over away from me to face the light of the window. I kissed the back of her neck and let her fall back to sleep. My place in our tiny bed was flat against the wall. I knew there was no getting up for me until she decided to do so. I didn't care. What could be better than lying next to her like this?

"I wish there were no work today," she said, sleepily.

"Yes, that would be nice, but it has to be done. We both know."

"Of course we know, and Robert will, of course, be there on guard to make sure we do."

"Robert is our boss, but he is no slave driver. He's a nice guy."

No answer. We were both awake. There was no alarm clock. We had no need of it. It was as if we worked together like a machine. I watched as she raised her left arm and took hold of the cover. I always knew what was going to happen next. It was part of our brief time in the morning together. Playfully, I tried to beat her at her own game. I already had half an advantage because my right arm was under her waist. As quickly as I could, I reached around the rest of her waist with my left arm in an attempt to stop her pulling at the cover and sending it flying to the floor. I succeeded, but it was for her a very competitive little moment. She punched the back of my hand quite aggressively and broke triumphantly away, taking the cover with her. She always won, and where was the harm in that? She padded her pretty little feet on the cold bare stone floor no more than the four steps' distance to our wash hand basin. Where there was only a single cold water tap. Our room was tiny, made even smaller by Vivvy's many possessions. There were books and records and binders containing her essays and articles, as well as numerous cuddly toys, and not forgetting lots of small, complicated pieces of girly equipment balanced in carefully chosen temporary alternative accommodations while we slept, their normal place of residence being the only possible one – piled on the bed, of course. It was the only place to sit as well as the only place to sleep! My few meagre things of no real value all fitted into the single duffel bag that I had brought with me. I watched her as she stood there by the window, naked in silhouette behind the drawn flimsy yellow curtains in the early morning light, washing herself with soap and flannel. She had the effortless ability of appearing differently at the various times of the day, but I think her early morning look was my personal favourite. She was achingly beautiful, so petite and vulnerable and lovable. But before I knew it, sadly for me, she was washed and dressed and ready to leave. We had to do it like this, because there was no room for us both at the same time. It was strange. She normally took a little longer. She hesitated at the door and turned in my direction. Then she looked at me, but her face was pinched, as if she was worried about something.

"Love, what's wrong?" I asked, staring back at her in the same way. I couldn't help it.

"What's wrong is that you have to leave, mate." I was puzzled. "Leave? Why do you say leave? We'll both go to work the same as we always do." She shook her head dismissively.

"Work isn't the issue, mate. You have to go back to prison and that's the end to it."

I sat bolt upright, bug-eyed, wide awake and back alone in the real world of my hospital bed. Andy and Paul stood next to each other. I'd got to know Paul quite well by now, and I could tell that, although he was good at hiding his feelings, he was not best pleased. I wondered if I had done something wrong. Nothing was registering with me. Andy, who made no effort to hide his feelings, was looking down at the floor.

"The thing is, mate, it's the press." said Paul, shaking his head ruefully, "I'm sorry. Yeah right, what you wouldn't do to 'em right now, hey? What they reckon is that if they can take a photo of you leaving here at the end of your sentence, they'll do a story of you saying you have never really been in prison, and that you misled the authorities to pull a fast one to get some money. Thing is, if they do that, the boss reckons that if they get away with it, you'll end up with nothing."

"But that's just plain ridiculous!" I felt like I was drowning. I think Andy was actually crying. "Why would they do that? And what about me? My health? How long have I got left?"

"I'm sorry, mate. We were all rooting for you, hoping you

would leave from here. What we all wanted, it was."

"And my time left?" I asked.

"Don't think you need to worry about that. Can't be that long, judging by how long *I've* been here," he chuckled. "And don't you worry about being inside, either. There's not a single perv that will dare to come anywhere near you this time. The boss made well sure of that. Got you the best protection you'll ever need, trust me!"

I knew Paul was trying his best to help me, but in spite of everything he was saying I had no confidence in any of it. I was reeling, trying and failing to get a grip on it somehow, and still coming round from a sleep that was unusually deep for me into the bargain.

"Your health is not too bad," Andy said in a low and unfamiliar voice. "We've done as much as we can to keep you here, but you'll be okay, health-wise." He returned his stare back to the floor. He was trembling.

"As long as we can get you out of here now," Paul said. "While it's dark, there's less chance of being spotted by those vultures."

Now, I was even more confused.

"Now? At night? How is it night? I haven't been asleep that long, surely!"

Andy looked up at me as if he was pleading with me.

"I'm so sorry, Mark, but it was the best thing all round! Please, you were agitated and we, that is, I, gave you a sleeping draught. Just to help you relax, that's all!"

"Andy? You lied to me! You told me that it was better that you didn't do that. It would show that I was in control of myself. That's what you said!" Now, I was upset as well. Welcome to the pity party, I thought.

"So, if you don't mind getting out of bed, it's time to go," Paul said, quietly, almost apologetically.

Andy was crying.

"I'm so sorry, Mark!" he sobbed, but he couldn't take a step forward, because Paul stopped him. He raised his arm to show me what he was holding. It was a coat-hanger, on which hung a clean set of prison clothes. Paul handed it to Andy, who in turn handed it to me, and then I myself took it from Andy. I looked around and remembered that I had not even thought about clothes for the entire time that I had been in this room. I looked at the prison clothes again. They looked like they had come straight from the dry cleaners, plastic wrapping and everything. I stared at them. What it represented struck me forcibly. On first coming into hospital, I had wanted to get as well as I possibly could as quickly as I possibly could to prove myself better than those pervs that had assaulted me, but as time passed, I had grown weary of it all. Now, I just wanted to go back home, collect what money they said was due to me, do those few repairs on my house, find a tenant and go back to France and that world that I had fallen so much in love with.

"Let me get you a coffee at least," Andy stammered, interrupting my thoughts. "You've been asleep, and it'll help." I watched him leave the room without looking at me. Strangely, without another word, Paul returned to his post outside the door in the hallway. Not long for him here now, I thought.

They had even switched my room's light out because I was

asleep. It was still out. The only light was from the corridor outside. Slowly, and with a heavy hand, I ripped open the flimsy plastic film and took out the clean and pressed prison clothes. I was right. They had been dry-cleaned. They even had that dry-cleaned smell. Slowly, I got dressed. When I was finished, I felt strange. I suddenly felt that I did not belong in this room anymore. I couldn't even sit down on the bed that I had occupied for so long. I simply stood there. Not so much to attention, but a fatalistic slouch. My shoulders sagged and my heart sank with them..

Eventually, Andy returned with two hot cups and some chocolate biscuits. He stopped still in the doorway when he saw how I was dressed. Silently, he put everything on the top of the bedside cabinet. He sat down on the unmade bed and signalled for me to come sit next to him. I did, this time feeling even more strange, as if I was visiting, somehow. He handed me one of the cups and put the biscuits on the bed between us.

"It really is too bad you have to go back, isn't it?" he said, not looking at me, but through the door to the corridor outside. I did the same, wondering what lay beyond it. I had no idea. I felt as if I had never been outside this room. I nodded.

"I want to tell them to stick their money so that I can go straight back home, but twenty thousand is something I just can't afford to turn down, you know?"

There was a pause.

"I don't get much time off, but I'll try to visit, I promise."

"That's okay, honestly." I said wearily, shaking my head. "I reckon you've already done more than your job on my account."

We fell back into silence, both staring in the same direction at the light in the corridor. It was a terrible feeling, just waiting for the inevitable. It hadn't been freedom in that hospital room, but the point is, it wasn't prison either. In a twisted way, you could say the two pervs in the kitchen had done me a favour. We sat there together, drinking hospital coffee and Nurse Andy wasn't making conversation anymore.

When he saw that I had finished my coffee, Andy took my empty cup and put it together with his back on the tiny bedside cabinet. Without standing, he straightened up and gave a loud and deliberate cough. Paul entered the room, carrying what I presumed, largely because of its rough appearance, was a prison-issue blanket. It was nothing like the bedding I had become accustomed to of late. This confused me. Were they so concerned for my well-being that they thought that I needed to be kept warm on my way out?

"Come on then, lad," Paul said, "let's go." Even he sounded reluctant. "Wait a minute, though!" he said again before I could as much as move. "Nurse? Can we get this man a wheelchair? I mean, I know he can walk, but he can't walk that far, can he?"

"Yes, that's right." answered Andy, his voice still shaky with being upset. "He's very weak. I'll go straight away." He sprung up from the bed where he was seated and rushed past Paul out into the light of the corridor. While he was gone, Paul was silent. I wish to this day that I knew what he was thinking right then as I watched him standing silently.

"Okay! Excuse me, please, gentlemen!"

Andy brought in the requested wheelchair. Slowly, I got

up and put my denim slippers on. Before I sat down in it, I turned around to Andy and extended my right hand.

"Okay, Andy? Thanks a lot, mate. Don't know what I would have done." Of course, he didn't shake my hand. He embraced me and sobbed as if I was family.

"I'll come and visit, I promise. Trust me." He looked up at Paul, his face wet with tears. "And you! You had better look after him after all he's been through!" he said, a little too fiercely for my liking.

"Don't worry, Nurse," Paul said. "No problem." He beckoned to me.

I sat down in the wheelchair and expected Paul to put the blanket over my lap or something, but he did not. Strange, I thought. Why had he possibly brought it? There was a pause; then Paul led the way out of the room. Because I was in a chair, it was sadly impossible to turn back for one last look. As we left the room, the full blast of the light hit me and I clenched my eyes closed for a while.

Leaving Hospital

The fact that we had taken a left turn was something I had particularly noticed, since I remember that Paul had sent the reporter scurrying off away from my room to the right. And, in the event, I had rightly guessed that this was the front of the building. I felt stupid and frustrated sitting in this wheelchair. We went silently along the brightly lit corridor for quite some distance, footfalls hardly making a sound, past many doors, and I was curious about what was behind each one of them. Having been in one single room for so long, this was the natural reaction. Then, up ahead to my left, we were approaching a café, and the sheer smell of it almost flattened me. It was so beautiful to see normal people getting on with normal lives and talking about normal things. A strong urge to get up and run seemed to rise up from inside me. But I remembered what I had been told, that in no time at all, I would be a normal part of society again myself. I decided that I would not tell Robert anything about any of this. I had no idea what I would in fact say, but I knew that I would have to start thinking about it. Ah! Plenty of time, I thought. Once I get back home and happily lose myself doing those repairs. I just knew that I was more than capable of piecing it all together, but there were far more immediate things on my horizon to be concerned about. Yes, the order of the day was definitely first things first.

The lift doors jolted open noisily. Paul looked around in all directions and we went inside. If I had read him rightly, he looked as if his every move might have been a risk he did not want to take. Once inside, he pressed the button for the Lower Ground Floor. To my surprise, it was no fewer than four floors down. The atmosphere was very tense. There were things I wanted to ask, but that was clearly impossible. Eventually, the lift came to a sudden stop and the doors opened. Once outside, Paul again looked all around to make sure the coast was clear. Then came a moment of uncertainty. There was a set of double doors straight ahead. Paul was not impressed, but shrugged his shoulders. He went to them, but didn't go through. He stood at their wired glass windows, and cupped his hands around his face. He peered out into the night while I waited for the result. It was obviously a success, because he came and pushed me forward. Then, again without a word, he threw the prison-issue blanket over my head. Once through the doors it was mercilessly cold. I shivered with the shock to my system. I was feeling weak and drained of energy, leaving me with little strength even to stand up. Fortunately, it was not long before I heard a vehicle approach. A door opened and I was quickly hustled inside, leaving the wheelchair behind. I was in the backseat with a guard to my left. The blanket was not removed, but I felt better for being out of the cold. I was still exhausted, but at least I was warm. I slumped forward, half asleep. As the car drove off, the silence was broken by the guard seated in the front seat beside the driver.

"Tell you what, right? We should definitely have been in plain clothes, tonight. And that goes for 'im in the back, too."

"What are you talking about?" asked the driver. "It's a piece of cake. The press aren't waiting to pounce on us. It's not that big a story for them anyway!" He gave a grunt, as if to indicate that this was his opinion, and that was that.

"No, no!" the guard in front insisted, "you don't know them. They're sneaky swines, all of them. They could be anywhere. Anywhere that there's a bunch of people to blend in with."

"Yeah, but that's only if they think it's worth it. And besides, we're still posted outside the hospital room. Make 'em think he's still in there. Once we get back, all he's got to do is walk away like it's the most natural thing in the world. Stroll back to his car all slow-like and that's it. Throw 'em right off the scent. They won't have a clue until it's too late."

"Sounds reasonable to me," answered the voice to my left. "Whatever you do, don't take that blanket off." he added, talking to me, obviously.

I nodded. This was something I totally understood. Besides, it felt warm. Then I wondered about my personal comfort when I reached my journey's end! Then suddenly, the car swerved violently to the left, then to the right and then to the left again with horns blaring. They shouted and swore, and the man to my left pushed me heavily with both hands down onto the floor directly behind the driver's seat and tried to do the same himself behind the passenger seat. I really had no idea at all what to make of all this. Was I so important that I justified this sort of attention? The deafening screech of brakes as the driver fought to hold on to the control of the car seemed unending, and yet, strangely I was not afraid. The driver stamped on the brakes again, this having the effect not of grinding to a halt and pressing me forward, but of gradually slowing down. In my opinion, there would have been nothing left of the tyres at this rate, otherwise! Well, I thought, he's doing well, considering we hadn't crashed or anything. Everything became relatively calm again. We were still moving. That was something. Surely, it wouldn't be long, now. I maintained my position, crouched down behind the driver. As the prison officers chatted away to each other about work and about their own schedules, customarily bewailing their respective lots, I felt that whatever emergency had arisen that had caused them to drive so madly was now over. One thing for sure, I was not going to ask them. I felt closed in, trapped and frightened. Believe it or not, I was looking forward to getting out! Yes, getting out from under this blanket, getting out from this car, getting out into some fresh air and to face head-on whatever was waiting for me!

Oh yes! Time to rejoin life again!

Prison. One More Time

The car finally came to a stop. Home sweet home, I thought. The guard on the back seat with me pulled the blanket off me. My head was down and my arms were above my head as if I was sheltering from a possible explosion. I straightened up, blinked and looked around.

"Okay, out!" the guard said before I knew what to do. I struggled up from behind the driver's seat and got out of the car. It was pouring with rain and as I got wet, the outside instantly made its presence felt. I looked down and saw that one of my slippers had come off and turned back to the door of the car to look for it.

"Come on! Stop lagging about!" the guard said, impatiently, and he and his partner grabbed an arm each and marched me inside to the entrance room, with only one slipper on. Now, I was soaking wet *and* freezing cold.

"Well well! Our famous guest returns!" sneered the duty officer. He slid a piece of paper towards me from under the glass in front of him.

"Your autograph, please, sir!" he said, keeping the same contemptuous tone of voice. Shivering with cold, I took the pen, signed my name and slid the paper back to him. He took the paper, compared it with another piece of paper on his desk, and when he was satisfied, got up from his chair. He yawned and stretched himself.

"It's okay. Bring him in."

"About bloody time, too. Go on!"

"That's one we're all glad to get over with."

"For sure!"

I was led through a large steel gate, which had a red light on either side. They walked me slowly through, and when they were satisfied that I was not going to set any alarms off, the duty officer locked the gate behind me. He looked at me and sighed.

"Come with me, your majesty. You're on watch. Special treatment for you, you see. Deputy Manager will see you in the morning if that's all right with you, of course."

I didn't answer. I was too tired, and it felt like he was baiting me to say something to get me into trouble, and trouble was definitely something I had no appetite for ever again in the rest of my mortal existence, thank you very much. I simply walked wearily with him on the cold hard floor to the watch cells. He stopped at one and took the keys off his belt and unlocked its door. To me, it looked a completely random choice. The door opened loudly, and I went inside quickly, not wanting to provoke his already bad mood. He held on to the door as I walked past him.

"Oh, and one more thing," he said, "while you're on watch, you're being filmed, so... keep your hands above the blanket, right?" he winked and closed the door. I collapsed on the bed, soaking wet, freezing cold and completely exhausted. But I didn't care anymore. With the lights still full on, I drifted away. My last pathetic thought on that first night back in prison as I fell asleep was that I missed Andy. He was a good man, and I wished I was back there.   But it couldn't continue, couldn't go on, and that was that.   Here I was again.   Back to the very place I first started.

Then came the morning after.   I had slept on the cell bed fully dressed.   It must have been a really deep sleep, because the bed was undisturbed around where I lay.   Neither did I dream.   The lights were on full beam again, but I didn't remember them either going out or coming back on.   And that was something worth saying because the lights in the watch cells are always that much brighter than everywhere else.   They have to be, I guess, if we're being filmed.   Lights, camera, action, right?   Not that in my case there's much to see.

There was a banging at the cell door, and I was ordered from outside to stand up and well away from the door, which of course I did without even thinking about it. The best way of doing things here.   Any rocking of the boat for any reason, even if it feels as if you have just cause for your actions, always results in life getting worse, not only for yourself but for everyone else.   And when it's discovered that it's you that started the ball rolling downhill, no matter how bad it gets for the other inmates around you, they will find a way of making your life a very nasty flavour of misery.

So, still half asleep and unwashed, I stood to as near to attention that I imagined attention to be in the far corner of the cell while a different duty officer brought in a stainless steel breakfast tray.   I wondered what mood this one was going to be in.

"You'd better be quick about eating this, because the Deputy Manager is coming in here to talk to you soon, so when he comes, you'd better be on your toes, you understand?"

"Yes sir. I understand," I answered. He sounded just as tired as I felt. His words may have been abrupt, but his manner was not. I was glad. I particularly noticed that he did not mention taking a shower. I then intended to content myself with a quick wash and brush-up. He paused at the door on his way out and looked me over. When he was satisfied that everything was as it should be, he stepped out into the corridor and closed the cell door behind him. As soon as he had gone, I sat on the bed next to the tray and went to the far end of the cell and put it down on the stainless steel table and sat down on the stainless steel chair. I carefully lifted the two lids and inspected the food by prodding it with the plastic fork provided. I did this just in case. I remembered that I had worked in the kitchens in this place, and I decided that if anyone was still there who felt in whatever way their mind worked that they had a score to settle, the only way that they could exact revenge now was by messing about with my food. I prodded and poked in every direction for a while, until I felt that the food was safe. Which indeed it was. I also remembered what the duty officer had said, essentially about there being not much time. In the event, this was not necessary as the one thing I had obviously forgotten was just how hungry I was. I couldn't comment on the quality of the meal, except to say that there was nothing wrong with it for the short time it took me to finish it. That done, I put the lids back on the plates and placed the tray to one side and washed my face and hands in cold water.

As soon as I had done this, it seemed to me, there was

another loud banging that brought me to my senses and I was told once more to stand away from the door. And so, once again, I stood away in the far corner to attention as the cell door opened. As I waited, two men entered. One was the duty officer and the other man, slightly portly and middle-aged, in a well-worn suit. It seemed to me that worn-out suits were the go-to choice for plain clothes staff here.

"Good morning, Mister Bashford. David Lewis. Deputy Prison Manager. Mister Barnett sends his apology but has some other business to attend to this morning," he said brightly, without trying to sit down. I nodded, and we shook hands. He turned over the pages on the clipboard he was carrying. "There are, as I'm sure you are aware, some problems with your presence here. Namely, your safety. Especially as the inmates who assaulted you are still resident, and have had their sentences lengthened as a consequence of their crime against you. Also, as a result of this prison administration's proactive appeal to the court, you have been granted compensation payable on your release, provided that you leave prison, not hospital. The reason for that stipulation remains as much a mystery to the management of this prison, including its legal advisors, as I'm sure it is to you. The only fortunate part of this whole scenario, as far as we are concerned, is the short amount of your own sentence remaining, that of three weeks. But we still remain concerned for your safety, nonetheless. Do you have any questions at all?"

"Yes I do, thank you, sir." I said, as politely as I could.

"Go ahead, Mister Bashford."

"Why can't they just waive my sentence and let me go

home? And what exactly can be done about my safety? Am I to stay in this cell for another three weeks after being in one room under guard in hospital? The Study Centre. What about that?"

He lowered the clipboard to his side.

"Well, as far as we can guess, and guesswork is all we have on this, we think it's a face-saving measure on the part of the court as a result of having to pay out compensation. The mindset being, all right, so we've lost, but that doesn't mean we have to make life easy for you because we still have to look like we're in charge. A pain, I know, but there you go. As for the Study Centre, I have to admit that there are a few teething problems with that particular project, so it's been put on the back burner for a while. However, we still have the old trusty library, don't forget." He paused, but he knew that I was not satisfied.

"Oh, yes, I'm sorry," he nodded, "with regard to your safety. Sadly, you will largely be in this cell for the remainder of your sentence, but not permanently, as in all day. You will be given full access to the prison library, as I say, such as it is. By way of something on a personal level, we have taken what you might regard as a somewhat unorthodox measure. Later today, the duty officer and I will introduce you to a man by the name of Ellis Robbins. Please don't be alarmed, but he is a fellow inmate. But I can safely tell you, based on the experience of witnessing this man for the entirety of my own time here, that you will be safe in his hands. He will be of enormous help to you, because he will be dealing with you the same as he has done with countless other inmates. By this I mean that he will act as a friend, counsellor and guard. As soon as his value became apparent, he was granted training and is fully accredited as an authorised voluntary prison visitor! He is a highly trusted and respected member of this community. Please have no fear of him. No one will come near you when you are outside this cell when they know that he is looking after you. There is one thing I will advise you on, though; for reasons he may or may not reveal to you, no one calls him by his name. Everyone calls him Dad."

I listened to all this carefully. I nodded once again. "Thank you, sir. When do I meet this man?"

"That will be after lunch today." He smiled at me in an attempt to reassure me. I smiled back. "Try not to worry too much about this, really." We shook hands again and both men left my cell, the duty officer taking the tray.

After they had left, I sat down on the bed. I looked around. This part of the prison was noticeably quieter than the hospital. Also, the door of that room was always open, and I could see people as they walked past, whether patients, visitors or staff. There was always something going on there, but not here. Here, there was only silence. Maybe if I felt that I had a lot to reflect on, here was the ideal place to do that, for sure. Eventually, I gave in to my weariness and lay back down on the bed, in spite of how worried I was.

What was so special about... Dad.

Dad

I was served another tray. This time it was a simple lunch. I was assured that the meals were all the same, but my presence here, although it would be known, was as of now out of the range of anyone who might feel inclined to settle any perceived score. In a short while, apparently, all this would be very plain and obvious to me. The only effect that this constantly repeated phrase seemed to have was to leave me with a rising sense of confusion, as well as worry. I ate my lunch in silence, put the tray on the far side of the stainless steel table and lay down on the bed again and slept.

For someone who was destined to change the whole course of my life, it was not much of an entrance. I was stood to what I guessed was attention and the three men came in. He stood in the middle, wearing the same prison clothes as myself, with the exception that he was wearing a plastic ID tag. It's a picture I have clearly stored in my head to this day.

"Mister Bashford," said Mister Lewis, "I have both the pleasure and the confidence to introduce you to your new companion and confidant, Mister Ellis Nathaniel Robbins, otherwise known to all and sundry here as Dad." He said this almost triumphantly.

"Glad to be able to meet you at last, Mark. I'm very sorry it's taken so long," said Dad, without extending his hand. He walked with a stick and was rakishly thin. His voice sounded like hot liquid poured on gravel, but what captivated me most was his stare. I was guessing, and quite rightly, that he was sizing me up. As he did so, I felt, ever so faintly as if from a distance, something I had not felt for a long time, and I had no idea why I was feeling it now. Rage. It was very weak, almost afraid, but there it was. Interesting, I thought. "Time we went for a walk, you and I, don't you think?" He looked around at Mister Lewis and the duty officer and waited for a response.

"He's in your hands now, Dad," said Mister Lewis, brightly, smiling and raising his hands.

"Just one thing, please?" I asked. "If I'm going for a walk, could I have some shoes and socks?" They laughed together.

They were simple mugs of coffee, and we simply faced each other on opposite sides of a table in the prison canteen drinking from them. It was not mealtime and we were alone. It was very relaxed. But it is common folklore that in prison, nothing is quite what it seems. Neither was it completely true that we were absolutely alone in the true sense of the word, because every now and then someone, either a cook or a KP would come out from the kitchen and perform some random odd job behind the serving counter, apparently taking no notice of us. Apparently.

And that was just the way Dad wanted it. "How's this working for you, then, Mark?"

"Don't know, really. All I know is, that I'll be glad to get back home, out of all this. Um, no disrespects, of course!"

"No offence taken." There was a sliver of a smile as he shook his head dismissively. Still sizing me up, are you, I thought. "Do you have any plans?"

"They're not grand plans or anything like that, but as far as it goes, I want to go home, do some repairs on the house, rent it out and go back to France to my old job, or one similar to it."

"Sounds good. Do you think you'll stick to it?"

"Yeah, of course. Why not?" He shifted awkwardly in his seat. "You see, it's like this, you may not realise it, but..." he took a breath through his front teeth. "This place. Prison. It changes people," he paused and looked around, then pointed straight at me. "Changes you."

"Well, I promise I'll be good from now on, honest!" We both laughed. He gently but emphatically placed his hands palms down on the table and looked me straight in the eye, and there was that stare again.

"Talk to me, son, if you really want to leave this place. Because trust me, I can see plain as day that you don't want to leave. You love it here just as much as I did the first time I was inside."

I couldn't break free.

He was talking bullshit and I wanted to tell him that he was talking bullshit. But for some unknown reason, I found myself unable to do that. I could feel myself trembling and I began to sweat. I wanted to tear him apart for talking to me like this, but I had taken special notice of the reactions of the other inmates and members of staff who had passed us as we had walked from the observation cells through to this canteen. Everyone looked terrified of him. Staff included. The thing is, he looked so frail. Why would they react like that? I tried to speak, but nothing came out. What had he done to me? He pursed his lips and shook his head. Still with the pointing.

"It's the rage, that's what does it. It starts with wanting to show that you're as good as they are, right?"

I nodded.

"Then you think you're going to get even; that some day you're going to visit vengeance upon those who have wronged you, but the rage is lying to you, you see. It's saying something but doing something else. Trust me, I know from experience. Its mission is to destroy you, and it will use all the smoke and mirrors it takes to do that. Take your plans, for example; your plans to return to France and work there and chat up all those pretty French girls. And when you get there, you'll live happily ever after. But it's all a lie, you see. Here's what's most likely going to happen. You'll collect your money from here and you'll go there, expecting to get your old job back, but it's likely there won't be any room for you just yet. But no problem, because, hey! you've got some money now and so you'll live it large for a while, but then, before you know it, the money will be gone and none of those pretty little French girls will want to know you and you'll feel oh so sad and lonely.

"Then you'll try to get your old job back again. This time you'll make more of an effort, but your old boss will see you all drunk and sad and burned out and he won't want to know you. He'll tell you that there is no job for you here, now mon ami. And that's when the rage will win, because that's when you'll see him as a smug old man and punch him square in the teeth and when he's down you'll keep punching and punching until he pisses his pants and you'll know he's gone, and you'll look down at him all bloody and dead, and then at your hands all bloody and broken, and then you'll hear the sirens, all loud and wailing, and you'll see the lights all blue and flashing, and that will be the end of you. But you'll be the winner, you see, because you'll be where you really want to be. Here. In prison. Safe. No more worries, and the rage will be the winner too. Oh yes! It will have you where it wants you and will most likely have the last laugh because you'll have planned it all very carefully right there in the back of your mind on your first day here.

"Yes, then the screws will put you on watch, but it will be you that will be watching them. And you'll be watching them and waiting for a time when you know that they won't be watching you. But that will never happen, you see. You'll learn that soon enough, but you'll try to top yourself anyway and fail and that is when you'll realise that you've been a failure at everything and there will be nothing left. You don't know what that feels like yet, and trust me, that is something you never want to experience.

"Now tell me, son, is that something you want? You want to know why they put me with you? Because I'm your last chance to face up to the reality that you need a plan. Not the one you've made for yourself, oh no. A real plan. A plan that involves the only thing in this world that works, a plan that will get you what you need to get out of here and stay out. Maybe you might think that you'll get out of here and meet the love of your life. You never know who you'll meet from one day to another on the outside, that's true, but you can just as easily do something stupid that will put you back inside. There's only one thing you need and that's money, but it only really works when you've got it by the ton, and what they've promised you is only a couple of ounces.

"So here's the deal and it's not an option. When you walk out of here, you will have a plan that is so big and so different that no one else in the world will have thought of it. You will work hard at this, very hard, because you need to impress me, and therein lies your problem. I'm not easily impressed, but then again I'm sure you have already guessed that. If you still don't believe me, ask anyone in here. You have just three weeks of your sentence left. Don't worry. You're completely safe here now. But you have only one week to come up with a plan that impresses me, or let's put it gently, leaving won't be an option. I trust we understand each other."

Those words changed the course of my life and they have been burned into my memory ever since.

Without warning, he spoke up again.

"Don't worry, Mark. Get to work. I'm sure there's a measure of genius in you. Nelly! Frank! I think Mister Bashford would benefit from your help in getting back to his cell." He smiled thinly without dropping the stare and picked up his walking stick. He got up, reached across the table and shook hands with me.

And still with the stare.

Then, from behind me came two of the most muscle-bound men I have ever seen. Without a word between them, they helped me up and walked me back to my cell as gently as if they were helping an old lady to cross the road. I don't really remember the walk back to my cell or the little ritual involved in entering it. I kicked off my boots. I covered my face with both my hands from the glare of the light.

He was right. The man called Dad was right. Esprit Fort, as I had called my rage. The man called Dad had seen it. Seen *him!* That piece of wood in my father's shed. What did I possibly think I was going to achieve? Did I think I was some criminal mastermind, like Moriarty or the Joker or something? But what was the answer? What was I going to do? What *could* I do?

What?

The Final Death Of Johnny Dollz

In my cell with its hateful bright lights that were never switched off, I felt like screaming. What was wrong with my original plan? I enjoyed being in France and wanted to return there, and now, when I leave, I will have the means to carry out some repairs on my house so that I may rent it out and return to France and speak to Robert and ask either for my old job back or something similar. Or even another job in another place working for someone else he might be willing to send me to, if it was no longer possible for him to employ me again.

I remembered my house with great affection. It would be wonderful going back there. I still slept in the back bedroom, where I had slept since I was a child, and that my trusty duffel bag was still lying there in the bottom of my wardrobe. I sighed and almost cried. I couldn't wait to go home! The man called Dad had no need to be concerned about me secretly wanting to return here. *Not at all!*

But his language was threatening. What else did "leaving was not an option" mean? What did he intend doing?

Suddenly, for no explicable reason, I was calm. I sat down at the foot of my bed and right there and then decided that I was going to go along with the flow. What harm could it do, after all? I would apply for a few jobs that I knew I wouldn't get, and maybe for a few training courses and business opportunities. In the details of it, it would completely depend on what was advertised. I would write up a plan and give it to him whenever he decided to ask me for it. After that, I would, of course, while away my remaining two weeks, collect my cheque and walk away without even looking back.

That was my plan.

Because I was in the observation block, all the cell doors were kept closed. I stood under the camera and pointed to the door and it buzzed and opened. I walked out in the direction of the library. No time like the present, I thought. It felt a little strange at first and I had no idea why, but this was a new experience for me. Like a double take, I was walking around the prison alone. It was almost like being free.

When I arrived at the library, Nelly was waiting for me. There was no mistaking who he was. Not just because I recognised him, but because he wore black jeans and a black t-shirt with the word "NELLY" in bold white letters across his huge chest. He sat there at the table facing the entrance for maximum effect, in total silence with his two trunk-like arms folded.

"Hello there," I said. I didn't find his presence in any way intimidating. He and his colleague Frank had been very helpful to me and had proved that they could be very gentle, but he definitely looked out of place as he sat in a library at a table without a book or a magazine in front of him.

"I thought I would get started right away."

No answer. I immediately wondered if he was mute. I asked at the desk for some newspapers and a pen and some scrap paper. The pen was given on the strict condition it was not to be taken from this room, and of the serious consequences of not doing so, and to be returned to the desk prior to leaving the library. I took a deep breath, gathered up the items I had requested, sat down at another table and started to work.

I was going to be methodical about it. On the largest piece of paper I drew a line across the top. On it I wrote the headings Date and Description, then started thumbing through the papers. The first steps had to be the normal and obvious ones; I applied for jobs. I wrote the relevant contact details that had been provided by each advert, the job I was applying for and the essential elements of what I would put in each letter. Sometimes it was requested to apply only by calling on the telephone. I gave these a miss. I wouldn't even mention these, because they were most likely small businesses who needed staff urgently. If Dad was aware of these and asked me why I didn't apply for any of them, I would make it very clear how unlikely it was that they would respond favourably to me when I told them that I was talking to them from prison. In all the letters, I would be using my home address. I wrote and wrote until I had applied for every job in all four papers, fifteen in all. When I had finished, I sat back in my chair. If I was going to do this, I would need some writing materials. Yet amazingly to me, I was not tired. I returned the newspapers to the librarian and asked if there were any magazines that I might look through, only to be told that the library would be closing in ten minutes. At this, I returned the pen politely. I walked away and smiled brightly at Nelly and held up my work to him.

"I've got quite a lot of work to do, and if I'm going to do it, I'm going to need some writing materials. Do you think Dad can swing that for me, please?"

Nelly nodded. I nodded back and walked back to my cell. The feeling of walking about like this was starting to make me yearn to go home. That desire for freedom was burning inside me. Strangely, I began to think that Dad was doing me a real favour. Keeping me busy like this was the best possible therapy. Perhaps he was not so insane after all, I thought. Perhaps he knew what he was doing. He was definitely unconventional; there was no doubt about that. He certainly thought "outside the box", but then that was exactly what he was trying to get me to do. Is that how he was with the rest of the men in here? Perhaps that is what it takes, just that. Who knows?

Imagine my sheer speechless amazement when, arriving back into my cell, I saw on my little stainless steel table, all neatly arranged, a supply of writing materials. There were two writing pads, a large packet of envelopes and, yes, a ruler, a black ballpoint pen, a pencil and an eraser. This was unbelievable. None of the last of these things were allowed, especially in the observation cells. Yet here they were, on my table as innocent as you like. Straight away, I stepped directly under the camera, even though I knew they could see me anywhere in the cell; it was just right to do exactly that. I raised both thumbs and mouthed the words "thank you".

I was so glad. I kicked off my boots for the second time that day, sat down on the little stainless steel chair at the little stainless steel table and started writing. I don't know how long I took, but I didn't stop until all fifteen letters were completed. I didn't seal the envelopes. I thought that Dad might want to read them, and besides, although no one had told me, wasn't there some sort of regulation about sending out letters from prison? Better safe than sorry on both counts, I thought. I relaxed and tried to get some sleep. The evening meal would be around soon. Tomorrow, I would concentrate on applying for training courses and some low-key business opportunities, as well as applying for more jobs. I drifted happily away.

I began the day after in a very happy frame of mind. After a contented night's sleep, I came to the conclusion that Dad was in fact trying to help me. After breakfast, I made my way back to the library. I made sure I was not carrying any writing materials. The last thing I wanted to do was to make trouble. Even if I was under Dad's protection, it didn't do to take advantage. This time it was Frank who was on duty.

"Good morning, Frank." I said, pleasantly.

Frank nodded. I was beginning to understand their way. Tomorrow I would simply nod to Nelly, and Nelly would simply nod back to me. I had that feeling that today was going to be a good day. I was in the library and had nothing to do all day but apply for jobs, join training courses and make my plans. All of these I would write down in minute detail and submit them to Dad whenever he asked to see me. I was going to get a lot done today.

Today there were both newspapers and magazines. I decided to pace myself. Rather than asking for all the newspapers and magazines at once, I took two of each at a time and worked through them with a fine-toothed comb. I left nothing out. My finely detailed record-keeping also continued. I could see that there was going to be far more to do tonight when I got back to my cell. Even Sheila the librarian smiled at me and wished me success. Yes, I was actually enjoying all this. I was riding high on the crest of a wave in a sea of optimism.

This time, yes, this time, nothing was going to go wrong.

Nelly and Frank did their thing silently. This morning they had used their maximum intimidation technique in the kitchen to make sure that none of my food was tampered with, even to the extent of driving a fork through the hand of Matthew Buck, now an inmate himself, when they discovered that he had put excrement in my gravy. This was a side of prison life I would never see and I was glad about it. But I didn't care anymore. If that is what it takes to keep me safe for the short time I had left to serve a sentence I should never have been given in the first place, then so be it, I thought. When Dad told me this, my own father came to mind. I told him the little I then knew about his war record, and he agreed that Hawkey would have had no problem dealing with these lowlifes.

I did a lot of work in the library. Lunch was the only meal that I ate in the canteen. When it was lunchtime, either Nelly or Frank would escort me there. It was something special. You would think that someone famous was visiting. As soon as they saw one of them, always going in first, each and everyone would get out of the way and a whole table would be cleared just for me. Nothing was too much trouble. I ate my lunch safe in the knowledge that nothing would intentionally go wrong, or there would be a special kind of hell to pay if it did.

That afternoon I returned to the library and I was as helpless as a rabbit caught in the headlights. I counted up the twenty-eight job applications, as well as the four training courses I was going to sign up for. There were as yet no emerging business opportunities within my reach. Besides, these were national papers and to apply for anything like these you had to be rich in the first place. But I did read through them, and my honest opinion was that if you can afford to take these on, you already don't need them. It just didn't make any sense. I suppose the real reason I slowed down was that I knew that there were already fifteen completed job applications in my cell from yesterday which had yet to be shown to Dad and posted, together with today's and the four extra training applications. It was going to be a lot of work sitting at the little stainless steel table, so I flipped through the papers to see the stories. Normally, it was all no more than passing interest, but I hadn't done this since I was in hospital and it seemed the right time for it now. I guessed I was becoming quite the news-hound. I was quietly enjoying this when suddenly I slammed on the brakes.

The Final Death of Johnny Dollz by Brad Coleman

The sad passing of rock star Johnny Dollz at the age of thirty-two was announced today to a waiting world by his agent Jake "Humanoid" Kane in front of the star's Los Angeles mansion. The death by drug overdose is being treated by local detectives and other law enforcement agencies as suspicious, as it happened whilst Dollz was in rehab and, as recently reported, making a steady recovery. His family, while thanking his vast multitude of fans and the public at large for their many messages of sympathy and support, ask to be given sufficient time and space to grieve and emotionally process their great loss. The gates of the mansion are already festooned with assorted flowers, messages and bric-a-brac. A date for the funeral has yet to be announced.

Dollz, real name John Pearson, always wanted to be a rock and roll star. His humble beginnings with a local band The Good Lovers toured local music clubs. But Johnny's dream was to fill whole ball parks with thousands of screaming fans and The Good Lovers just didn't cut it for him. His departure marked a huge leap in his evolution into the icon we remember here. After trawling local bars for musicians with dreams, he finally found the two men who with him formed the line-up he knew would work. Earl "Stick Man" Gilliam on drums and vocals, and Travis Witt on bass guitar and vocals. They were only two, but the three stuck together and became the legends we all know and love.

Initially giving themselves the name Teenage Pimp in an attempt to gain access to the up and coming Glam Rock scene, they soon dropped the name and stuck simply with Johnny Dollz. It was a wise move. They were noticed while performing an open-air gig at a local parking lot and signed a deal with Black Jet Records and soon released their first album, Doll City. It sold enough copies to get to number fifty-six in the charts. Not bad for an unknown band, but hardly world-changing. Their second album, Doll House, fared better. This may have been because it was released internationally, this time rising to number eighteen in the charts. But it was the infamous third album, Sex Doll, released only nine months ago, that rocketed Johnny Dollz to fame, and his two previous albums together with it. The album was roundly condemned as nothing more than pornography. And this was exactly what Johnny had planned, but Johnny was no fool. Embedded in the album was a song entitled "Can't Hide

Forever". It was released as a single and with the song "You Rock My Everything" on the B-side (this song was not on the album), not only proved that Johnny was one hell of a power ballad singer, but these were regarded as his best songs. The single and the album sold out, and so did the tour. No one could even get near him. But success led to the inevitable excess and unrestrained hedonism. And it was to LA's infamous night club, Meltdown City that the first responders were called to rush Johnny to his third and final visit to rehab after a three-night- straight bender. It was Jake Kane, his agent, who was the last person to see Johnny alive. He told the waiting media that Johnny wanted with all his heart to be free of drugs. This was, of all his many mistakes in his all-too-short life, without doubt the biggest. While recovering for the third time, he had written two songs: one depicting how defenceless the addict is, entitled "Your Victim", and the other describing how impossible it feels to escape, entitled "Buried Alive". Kane intends to release the voice recording made at the rock star's bedside as a single, not only as a tribute to Johnny, but also to raise money for local rehab clinics. As part of ongoing tribute, we print the refrain from the song Buried Alive:

I'm not dead I'm buried alive,
Hear the bell ring as I pull the string.
I'm not dead I'm buried alive,
Set me free, Set me free, Set me free.

John Pearson aka Johnny Dollz. 1953 - 1985.
Rest In Peace.

I had stopped and read this article because it was about Vivvy's favourite rock star, and it was, of course, sad to hear of his death. It also brought Vivvy back to mind very clearly. She would listen to his records on her primitive pink record player with its scuffed edges. But there was something nagging at me. I have explained that I had kept records of my activities on paper so that I could tell Dad exactly what I had done when I went to see him. I hastily consulted those records again to refresh my own memory. It was not the many jobs that I had applied for that concerned me now. No, it was the training courses that I was interested in. I had decided to go down the white-collar route simply because that was where the money was, or so I was led to believe. And besides, having now worked in a kitchen, and been filthy and sweaty at the end of every day, for me it was a far better deal to go to work clean and smart and to come home in exactly the same state. Far better. So I had applied for two courses for work in the financial and banking sector, and two courses in the insurance sector.

Yet still, there was something bothering me. I had had serious misgivings about them because the application forms had put doubt in my mind by creating an uncertainty by way of a line of personal questions. Essentially, I was asked to summarise what I felt I could bring to my work that was different, and how did I intend to stand out. I didn't know at that time the purpose of these questions and could not at that point remember my first attempt at answering them, but they had left me feeling inferior and uncertain. How could I possibly know what I would contribute to a job I had never done before? I had people skills and an eye for detail, but there was also to me the contradictory ideas that on the one hand I had to be a team player and on the other to be individual and quite clear about what it was that I could bring to the demanding tasks ahead that was unique to me.

But there was something about the newspaper article that seemed to light a fire in me. The worm of discontent squirmed in me and woke up Esprit Fort, but strangely in a good way. I began to think that my individual contribution was essential, but had not an earthly clue as to what that could or indeed would be. Maybe, just maybe, I thought, the questions and my emotional reaction to them were a good thing. Prior to them, I was simply doing what was asked of me out of fear of Dad, and making a big effort to show that I meant it. Then I thought that the training courses would show that I was coming at it from more than one direction, not content to leave one stone unturned as it were. As Esprit Fort grew stronger in me, my eyes widened. I looked down at the newspaper again and scanned the article. Was it because I was missing Vivvy so much that I was feeling like this? True, I did miss her. She was beautiful, and I had loved everything about her. In a sense, it would have been much simpler had she been the centre of my attention right then, but no. She was not. I looked down and scanned the newspaper article yet again. Dad had said that I should think differently to everyone else, and my own father was a fighter and had bought a house for cash and supported his wife and son simply by doing something that he saw needed to be done that no one else was doing and went ahead and did it. He didn't question it, just did it without stopping to think of what anyone else would think either of him or what he was doing, and it had worked for him. My trouble had been that from inside a prison, you're always asking the question why. Why did I do something so stupid to land myself in here? Why didn't I do the honest thing? And on it goes. Why, why. why. And that's the fatal question that, although it may not have made me a loser, will for certain keep me a loser. These forms had asked me the right question. It was the question that was going to get me out of here and keep me out. It was the question what! I had not looked up from the newspaper. My heart was beating like a piledriver and I was trembling with excitement. But at what? I read the article again and again.

The librarian looked across at me with a concerned expression on his face, but I took no notice because I felt that if I broke my concentration I would miss something important. I had also failed to notice that desk staff had changed. It grew in me that I absolutely knew that I was reading the answer but did not know what that answer was. My frustration was mounting. I sat back in my chair and tried to calm down, but still didn't look up. It was as if I was afraid to look up. I wanted all my thoughts to come to mind one by one, almost independently. This rock star had made it to the top by refusing to accept the inevitable. He had a dream and went after it with all his strength. He had cleaned himself out of drug addiction twice and was reported as making a steady third recovery. Never say die, heh? Good for him! Then, perhaps to process his experience in his mind, maybe even to scream at his lot, he had written two songs. I sighed and shook my head. No. None of this was relevant to me. Whatever the answer was, I just couldn't see it.

I looked up. I admit that I was almost in tears with anger and frustration. What calmed me down was when I remembered the tiny room I shared with Vivvy. She was so pretty. Especially when she was sad. I wondered if she was quite well off now and working in her favourite village for a magazine through the post and another job in either a restaurant or hotel. I sighed again. I wish I knew where!

I looked down at the newspaper again and there it was, as plain as day. I'm not dead I'm buried alive, Hear the bell ring as I pull the string. I'm not dead I'm buried alive.

Set me free, Set me free, Set me free.

The answer.

I could hardly breathe. I was grinning like a lunatic. I was wide-eyed with excitement. Esprit Fort was bubbling through my veins. The newspaper was now crumpled in my fist. I stood bolt upright so fast that I sent my chair toppling over behind me. At the sound, the librarian looked over at me, and Nelly got up and turned and faced me.

"Nelly!" I shouted. I couldn't help it. "Please take me to see Dad!" Nelly shook his head. I was horrified. Then his face changed. He actually smiled, and nudged his head backwards towards the door. I think my madman grin actually widened. I punched the air triumphantly and gave out a huge yell.

I *was* going to change the world and get insanely rich doing it!